MW00412172

SLEEPING
SECRETS

A Novel of Romantic Suspense

By
G.G. Vandagriff

Dedicated to my brave and beautiful sister
Beth ("Buffy") Gibson Haglund
1953–2018

CHAPTER ONE

Spring, Chicago, Illinois

Paula was sitting in her cubicle at television station WOOT when the call came.

"Am I speaking with Paula James?" asked a man with a deep, husky voice.

"You are. My assistant said you are a Federal Marshal?"

"I am. Ronald Sutherland. Based in Orange County." He paused. "Do you remember me? I knew you when you were a little girl."

His voice struck a chord deep inside of her. A chord that sounded safe and warm, filling her with a kind of peace she didn't ever remember feeling, except when David had his arms around her.

"Your voice sounds familiar to me," she said. "But I should tell you I don't really have any memories from when I was young."

"Oh." He paused for a beat. "Perhaps that is a good thing."

"Are you calling to tell me that I am in Witness Protection?" she asked. "How did you find me?"

"Your parents told you then?"

"No. The FBI did."

He cleared his throat. "I saw you on the news the other night. Very impressive work. Congratulations on taking down Magnus O'Toole. It was certainly time someone did."

"Thank you." Paula's stomach was in a knot.

"I was very sorry to hear of the murder of your father. I believe your mother has also passed away?"

"Yes," she said.

"You *are* in WITSEC. But after appearing on national TV, I worry that your cover may be compromised. You are the image of your mother. There are still people you may be a threat to."

Now her whole body knotted up. She crossed her arms over her middle and crossed her legs. "Someone still wants to find me? After all these years?"

"I think for the sake of your safety, especially considering the recent publicity, that you and I need to have a conversation. I would like to fly out to see you."

Paula didn't know how to respond. The FBI had told her there was a flag on her file noting that she was in witness protection, so she wasn't completely unprepared. But only the U.S. Marshals had the details.

Now, however, the idea of learning about a past she didn't remember daunted her. Though she missed her parents, she was contented with her life just as it was. A major shift in her reality would be an emotional earthquake. She didn't even know her real name.

"Ms. James?"

"I suppose I need to know," she said finally.

"For your own safety, if nothing else," the marshal said. "Would Thursday be convenient for you?"

Today was Tuesday. Upending her world just two days from now would be totally weird. *Come on, Paula. You're an investigative journalist. Digging is what you do.*

"Thursday is fine."

"How about if we meet at noon in the restaurant on the top of the Hancock Building? I've always enjoyed the view from there."

"All right. Thank you for coming to me. I hope your flight is tolerable."

"I'll see you then," he said. "Goodbye."

* * *

"He's coming on Thursday," she told David van Pelt over lunch at their favorite bakery. She had no appetite, but she was doing her best to eat a chicken sandwich on a croissant.

David was looking impossibly handsome today in spite of the sling. He wore a slate blue shirt that matched his eyes, He surveyed her with concern. "Are you ready for this?"

"I don't know, to be honest." She ignored her sandwich and shredded her napkin. "I know we said we were going to investigate it, but I'm getting cold feet. He says he needs to tell me for my own safety. That when I was on TV, he could see that I looked just like my mother. People are still looking for me, and he thinks they'll figure out who I am if they watched the news."

"Hmm. You have me wishing I was as good with a Glock as you are."

She smiled a little. "Hopefully, it's not going to come to that."

She adored David, but he was just coming off of a broken engagement, and she had considerable baggage of her own, so they were taking things cautiously. With his heavy dark brown hair, square jaw, and killer smile, he looked great on TV. He had made a name for himself as an investigative journalist. And now, as his partner, she was doing the same.

"Maybe I should look at it as an opportunity," she said, sitting up straighter.

"And maybe we're going to find out what's behind that stubborn door in your mind." Reaching across the table, David interlaced their fingers. "You're not ten years old anymore. And you just took down a vicious mob boss and saved my life. I have no doubt you can handle this."

* * *

Paula loved the Hancock building. It was the northernmost skyscraper on the Miracle Mile on Michigan Avenue. After growing up in sleepy southwest Missouri, she adored Chicago. Being part of the investigative team at WOOT TV had been a goal of hers since she'd graduated with her master's degree in journalism at Northwestern. Right now, she was very happy with her place in the world and not anxious to have it disturbed by what she knew would be scary revelations.

As she rode the elevator to the 99th floor, she adjusted the collar of her blouse under her yellow linen suit.

Everything is going to be all right. David is right. You are not ten anymore.

When she arrived in the restaurant, for once, she didn't even look at the view. Instead, she asked the hostess if her party, a Mr. Ronald Sutherland, had arrived.

"No. Not yet. Would you like to be seated?"

"Please."

The hostess led her to a window overlooking Lake Michigan. Paula ordered a Coke and sat watching the sailboats without really seeing them. She had expected the Federal Marshal to be here. It was noon on the dot. Perhaps he had been held up in traffic.

What is my real name? How did I get the scars up my arm and leg? Why do dark, enclosed spaces frighten me? Why can't I remember anything before we lived in Missouri?

There would be a certain relief in learning these answers. Paula was so lost in thought, she hardly noticed the time passing, until the waitress came up, nodding toward her menu.

"Would you like to order while you wait for your friend?"

Looking at her watch, she noted it was twelve thirty.

"Just another Coke, please. And maybe some bread?"

She waited, growing progressively more anxious.

By one o'clock, she had eaten all the bread in the basket. She should have given the marshal her cell phone number. What if he had missed his flight? What if it had been canceled? Probably the best thing to do was to go back to the station where he knew how to get in touch with her.

* * *

When the day passed at work without any further communication from Marshal Sutherland, Paula was very concerned. Slated for the early evening news, David told her to take the train by herself to Winnetka and pick up his car in the parking lot. He gave her his her his keys.

She arrived home to find her toy Yorkie anxiously awaiting her outside in David's back garden. Scooping him up, she gave him some love. She unlocked the door to the servant's cottage that the former owner of David's house had converted into guest quarters. She needed to find another place to live, now that she had a job. However, she knew she would miss the proximity to David, and she certainly could not afford to live in Winnetka.

After she had showered and changed into jeans and a long-sleeved tee, she made a quick stir-fry and sat down to work on her father's bills which had been forwarded from their address in Missouri. Petey curled on her lap and napped. Her cell rang. David. Was he at the train station already? The time said it was right in the middle of the news broadcast.

"Paula. I only have a second. Take Petey and go. No time for packing. I'll meet you at the Hampton Inn in Evanston. Take my car."

Before she could reply, he cut the connection.

What in the world?

Her heart beat in great thumps of dread as she grabbed Petey and put him in her bag. She also took her laptop and Glock, and then raced to David's BMW parked right outside her door.

CHAPTER TWO

She was sitting on the bed in her motel room with Petey on her lap watching Jeopardy, his favorite show when she heard the knock on the door. She jumped up to answer it. Peeking through the peephole, she made certain it was David.

When she opened the door, she saw that his brow was drawn with worry.

"Have you seen the news?" he asked as he strode into the room, urgency in every step.

"No. What's wrong?"

"Sit down."

She sat in the chair by the window, a feeling of dread clenching her stomach. Petey hopped back in her lap. "Tell me."

He pulled the other chair around the table, so it was next to hers. Taking her hand, he held it in his lap.

"The body of your Federal Marshal was discovered this morning. Shot in his hotel room at the Airport Marriott."

"What?" Paula sat up straight and took her hand back. She couldn't take in what he said. "Shot?"

"In the forehead. Security cameras on the floor and in the elevator were all spray-painted. They have no leads, honey. I'm so sorry."

Her head was swimming. The man whose voice had made her feel safe was gone. Probably because of her. She leaped up and raced for the bathroom where she was sick. Kneeling on the floor in front of the toilet, she couldn't seem to get to her feet.

He was someone important in my life. He knew I was in danger, so he flew all this way to get to me. And he was shot.

David knocked on the open door and entered. "I'll get you a glass of water. This is a horrible shock."

Once she had drunk the water and had gone in to lie down on the bed, he continued. "I'm afraid you're in danger, Paula. Whoever these people are, they know you're in Chicago. No files were found with the body. They know all about you, but they don't

5

know how much you know about them. I'm thinking they probably saw you on the news like the marshal did. As soon as I realized that, I knew they'd come looking for you at WOOT."

"So we're off the grid again?" Before she had been prepared. But this time she had felt safe, secure.

"I'm afraid so."

A new reality hit her. "David, they know who I am, but *I* don't know who I am. I don't even begin to know the why or the who in this situation."

"Federal Marshals protect witnesses specifically against drug traffickers, terrorists, and organized crime. So that gives you a lot of 'whos' to choose from."

"I've got to think." She put her fingertips to her temples. "I still have my Ellen Templeton ID."

"I talked to Mr. Q. He's good with me investigating this. So we're on the clock, and we can both disappear. You're not doing this alone." He sat beside her on the bed and drew her up into his arms.

After a moment of gathering strength, she straightened up and said, "Thank you, David, but the last thing I want to do is put you in danger again. You nearly got killed last time."

"Do you honestly think I could let you go this alone? Especially when you're so handicapped from lack of information?"

Paula's feelings were so conflicted; she felt unable to take even the first step away from danger.

Is there now any way I can find out who I am supposed to be running from and what my parents witnessed that put them into WITSEC?

Who killed the marshal?

Will I ever be safe unless I expose them?

Will my memories ever come back?

How can I expect David to follow me into this life on the run when he is still suffering from the wound that nearly killed him?

Right now, the last question felt the most critical.

"David, how are you feeling? Please be honest with me," Paula said.

"I have a follow-up with a doctor here in Evanston tomorrow. But I'm sure I'm fine."

"You had five-hour surgery to remove a bullet from your chest less than a week ago. At the very least, you have got to be exhausted. You shouldn't even be back at work yet."

"All right. Let's put it this way," he said. "If you go off without me, I will be in worse shape worrying about you than I will if you just let me tag along."

"These are murderers," she reminded him.

"How about this? We find a nice quiet place to hang out for a week or so and look into your parents' case. There has got to be someone in the marshal's office in LA who knows what's what. There has to be a computer record of your file for one thing."

She sighed. "You are incorrigible."

"Let's at least see what the doctor says. I'm sure I'll be fine. We send our assistants into our houses tomorrow to pack some clothes and computers and stuff. Then we rent a car under your pseudonym and take off somewhere. You can even drive if you want."

"All this hinges on what the doctor says. And I'm going with you to the appointment, so don't think you can keep anything from me."

"Agreed."

"Okay."

He grinned like a little boy whose Mom said he could have ice cream before eating dinner. Holding up a hand for a high five, he said, "In another life, I would have been a Navy SEAL. I'm indestructible."

She rolled her eyes. "That makes me shudder to think about."

"We're in funds. Mr. Q reauthorized our prepaid credit card and sent me home with some cash."

"Great. Hand it over, and then we'll order you a pizza in your room. You did get your own room, right?"

"I think you'd be safer if I stayed with you."

"Nice try.

"Have I ever said that you're cute when you're bossy?"

"Don't push it, van Pelt. I'm not in the mood."

CHAPTER THREE

He started his inquiries the day after he took out the marshal, but the TV station claimed not to know where Blythe Kensington lived. Of course, he had used her WITSEC name, now that he knew it. Paula James.

Norris, the cop he was working with in Chicago PD hadn't been able to turn up a car registration for her. He determined from the file he had taken from the marshal that she had been relocated to Lawrence County, Missouri after the trial. After instigating a search in that state, Norris reported that she had a white Honda Civic. The cop put out a BOLO on that car, but it wasn't until near midnight that they heard it was now in a ghetto on the south side. Probably stolen.

Beating the wall of the closet-sized office he was using, he finally reconciled himself to the fact that this wasn't going to be easy. He canvassed car rental agencies, but no one had rented to James.

In the meantime, Norris had been unable to trace the woman's address through Cook County utilities. Was she a ghost?

Tomorrow he was going to have to find some way of learning more about her life as Paula James from the TV station. He wasn't handsome, but he wasn't ugly either. Women usually talked to him.

CHAPTER FOUR

David did not sleep well. He was more than a little anxious about his doctor's appointment. He felt an urgency to get Paula out of the reach of the Marshal's killer. With her hair, newly blonde, swinging around her fragile-looking face with its high cheekbones, perfect nose, and Scarlett Johansson mouth, she looked like she needed protection. But it was she who had saved his life.

Discomfort visited him just below his breastbone, and it wasn't from his wound. Hadn't he just proved himself to be the worst kind of cad by the way things had gone down with Sherrie? Were these "knight errant" feelings real? Or did they spring from some kind of male biological imperative: save the woman and conquer her?

Paula was very capable and very bright. She could probably save herself a lot better than he could. She carried a mean Glock, and he was wounded for crying out loud!

But she had just been through several weeks of high-adrenaline detective work while on the run. Following that was her first week of appearances on the WOOT news and the ensuing stories about the meth bust that had turned into a national story.

Now she was faced with a multi-faceted threat of a different variety. A threat that had the potential to turn her world upside down in addition to the very real threat upon her life. His first reaction was to take her to Nova Scotia and hide her in a little fishing village where it was still winter. Maybe in a lighthouse. And . . . Well, maybe he shouldn't let his mind go there.

* * *

Dr. Pruitt was a short, balding thoracic surgeon who had taken over David's case from the doctor in Arkansas who had performed the life-saving surgery on David the week before.

"The surgery site itself looks good, but I'd like to do an ultrasound of the area of your injury, just to make certain your lung and blood vessels are healing properly," he told him. "You're still taking the antibiotics?"

"Yes."

David crossed his fingers, but the ultrasound looked good.

"You need to avoid any activities which may stress your lung tissue or the blood vessels which are still healing. No running or heavy exercise. How is your sleep?"

"Not the greatest, but I'm sure it will settle down."

Dr. Pruitt pulled a little card out of the drawer of the exam room. "Here are a couple of meditation and relaxation apps you can put on your phone. Use them to help you when you first go to bed. Insomnia is common after the kind of trauma your body has been through."

David was glad he had something tangible he could show Paula that would satisfy her need to mother him.

"I want to see you back here in two weeks, and we'll do another ultrasound."

He pretended to agree, though he had absolutely no idea where he would be in two weeks.

Entering the waiting room a few moments later, he gave Paula a thumbs-up. "I'm doing great." He told her about the ultrasound and showed her the card with the apps. "These are to help me with sleep. You should probably use them, too."

"Good idea," she said. "I'm so glad you're doing well. Our admins should have our stuff after lunch. They are meeting us at O'Brien's."

* * *

During his tossing and turning the night before, David had decided on a place to go to ground. "Indianapolis," he said during their traditional corned beef lunch. "Only a few hours away. Right on the Interstate. Good Internet and cell reception. I've already made a reservation in a suburb. They had a two bedroom suite."

"Sounds great," she said. "At least this time we're not running from law enforcement, so we can use our phones."

"Our phones are going home with Jill and Liz. We can't take anything for granted. The people chasing you could have resources in law enforcement. Someone knew about the marshal coming here, sweets."

She groaned.

They surrendered their phones to their assistants who brought clothes, toiletries, and laptops. Liz, Paula's assistant, had volunteered to keep Petey for the duration since they didn't know what lay ahead. David watched Paula hand him over with what he could tell was a pang.

Their first stop after renting a family-sized minivan in the name of Ellen Templeton was to a big box store to buy several burner phones. The trip to Indianapolis was uneventful. David actually dozed which was embarrassing. He only hoped he didn't snore. He woke up for their arrival.

"This town is heaven," said Paula. "Look at all the brick stores and streets and stuff. And there are flowers everywhere."

One of the things he loved about Paula was her ability to see the beauty and make the best of every situation. He used his phone to locate the B & B and gave her directions. The Brick Street Inn proved to be a light gray clapboard building with blue trim.

"Perfect!" said Paula. "This won't be a hardship, by any means."

David was pleased with his choice, but his chest was hurting. He had declined to wear his sling that morning, and now he was regretting it.

Their rooms were oak paneled as was most of the inn. Paula insisted on carrying the two duffels their assistants had packed, while David carried his laptop. They had registered as Mr. and Mrs. Dale Templeton.

"I'm going to take a nap," said Paula, to his relief. "I didn't sleep well last night."

It ended that they both slept until sunset. David was awakened by the shower running between their rooms. He felt stiff and sore but resisted pain pills. As he had explained to Paula on another occasion, they made him goofy and amorous.

He was determined to restrain himself where Paula was concerned. While she was dealing with such huge personal issues, it was no time to be pursuing her. She was vulnerable, and he knew better than to take advantage of that vulnerability. At least he thought he did. Seeing her showered and dressed all in black with her shiny blonde hair in a sophisticated bun, he wanted nothing more than to kiss her senseless. Fortunately, it was time for dinner.

The restaurant was upscale and homey at the same time. Fresh flowers sat at each linen-covered table. They both ordered steak and baked potatoes.

"So, have you heard from Sherrie at all?" asked Paula when their salads were served.

He gave a rueful laugh. "When all the publicity came out about our adventure, she was very repentant. She was determined to reinstate our engagement. It made me see her in a whole new light."

"I can imagine. You're the local hero. Who doesn't want to marry a hero?"

"Well, she didn't want to marry me when I was investigating. She likes the outcome, but not the process. I don't think that makes her the wife for me. To tell you the truth, I now wonder if my feelings for her were even authentic. I am the worst kind of cad, sweets. I should warn you—whatever you do, don't take me seriously."

Though he genuinely meant his words, she just laughed them off. "In her defense, it would be hard to be married to a man who was getting shot all the time."

"I suppose women like it better when men are accountants," he said.

She grinned. "That depends upon the woman. And the accountant."

Could he help it that his heartbeat sped?

After a generous dinner, David felt like he could go right back to sleep, but he resisted, deciding to call Jill, his admin, instead.

"Oh! David, I'm so glad you called. Poor Miss Sutherland has been trying to find Paula all day."

"Miss Sutherland? The marshal's daughter?"

"Yes. She's here in Chicago making the arrangements for her father. She says she knew Paula when they were girls back in California."

"Here," he said. "You'd better talk to her."

Going out of the room, he gave Paula privacy. As far as he was concerned, this was a great bit of news! The sooner they had this mystery solved, the sooner she would be out of danger.

The idea of Paula being at the mercy of whoever shot the marshal was making him crazy. He had seen the scars on her left arm. They went from her wrist to her shoulder. She had told him she had similar scars on her left leg. She had no memory of how they were inflicted, but she did remember painful physical therapy after they moved to Missouri.

She had also recalled being kept bound and gagged in the dark, and some terrible thing happening to her afterward. Fortunately, she couldn't remember the terrible thing, and he hoped she never would.

David had mixed feelings about Paula getting her memories back. He didn't know what it would be like for an adult to revisit a childhood trauma. Would she revert to her powerless childhood terror? Or would she be angry with those who had inflicted it, empowered by the fact that she was now an adult with options? What role would she expect him to play?

He knew he should encourage her to be independent. But, for whatever reason, he felt compelled to protect her.

CHAPTER FIVE

"Meet Blythe," Paula said as she walked into the cozy little sitting room. "Unfortunately, I still don't have a last name."

"It suits you," said David. "I like it. Are you going to keep it?"

Paula sighed. "I don't know yet. There is a kind of sacred feeling that that was the name my parents chose for me. Who knows who chose the name Paula?"

"So you spoke to Miss Sutherland?"

"Janice. Yes. I found out a few things." Paula sat on the ottoman that belonged to David's chair. She was still a bit overwhelmed by the new revelations. "She didn't know a whole lot, because she is just my age, but her father introduced us while my family was going through the trial. She thinks now that he probably thought having a friend would make me more relaxed."

"Did she remember where you lived?"

"We lived at the beach, she said. We used to make sand castles together. She liked it because she lived inland. Her father used to bring her on days when he was off work."

"If it was during the trial, maybe that was where your safe house was," said David. "You would have been in protective custody. You probably wouldn't have been allowed outside very often."

"Maybe I was only allowed on the beach because he was with us," she said. "She couldn't remember my last name. But, she remembered one thing kind of in retrospect." Paula clasped her hands tightly. "Whenever they were going home from a visit with me, her father always used to tell her that if anyone she didn't know tried to talk to her or asked her to get into his car, she was supposed to tell him no and run away. Even if he said, her parents had sent him. She remembers because it scared her to death every time he brought it up." She bit her lip hard. It wanted to tremble. "I was wearing a bathing suit. She saw my scars. She said they were scary, too."

"We need to call the marshal's office tomorrow and see if there are any backups of those files her father brought. There must be something on a computer somewhere."

"How are you feeling?" she asked. "I hate that you are worrying about me when you should be recovering peacefully in your own home."

"I don't do 'peaceful.' You know me. If I were home, I would still be stirring up trouble somewhere."

She felt his forehead. "You don't have a fever, at least. Are you taking antibiotics?"

"Faithfully, I promise."

"And pain meds?" She grinned as she asked the question.

"You know me and pain meds. I'm making do with over the counter stuff. It's really not too bad, sweets. I promise."

"Well, I think we need an early night. Didn't you tell me your doctor gave you some relaxation app?"

"Yeah." He found the card in his wallet and handed it to her. She loaded the app onto her phone.

"I hope you have a more peaceful night tonight."

"You, too."

He cupped her face in his hand and gave her a gentle kiss. Paula knew that anything more would have set her burning and she would have gone up like straw. She was way too needy right now. She pulled away reluctantly.

"Blythe," he said. "You know, I like that name. Was your mother a theater buff?"

"Yes. She graduated from Northwestern in the Oral Interpretation of Literature. It was all about poetry and theater. Why?"

"There is a play by Noel Coward: *Blithe Spirit*. A comedy about a clairvoyant."

"I wish I were clairvoyant. It would be a real advantage in this situation," she said with feeling.

"We'll figure it out. We already have one pretty convoluted case to our credit."

She was looking at him as he spoke, but now she looked away. She was afraid he would read the depth of the feelings in her heart.

"You're right," she said. "You know, I'm sorry you got shot, but I'm glad you're with me in this. It's pretty heavy stuff."

"I wouldn't let you take it on alone." He embraced her with his good arm and kissed her again. Even a gentle kiss warmed her through. She pulled away.

"Good night, sleep tight," she whispered and got to her feet.

* * *

In her bed, she curled into the fetal position.
Were you kidnapped then, Blythe?
What caused those horrible scars?

Something had caused her to retreat into traumatic childhood amnesia. Though it was horrible to contemplate, kidnapping made sense.

Pulling back the t-shirt she slept in she studied her scars. What kind of fiendish hell had she been through? Had she finally found the explanation for why she had never been able to remember her life before living in Missouri when she was ten?

Was the kidnapper still at large? Was that why the marshal had been killed when he had decided to come and tell her about the past "for her own safety"?

It made sense in a way. If, as she supposed, she was kidnapped to prevent her parents testifying in a trial, the defendants were probably in jail. Someone on the outside must have kidnapped her. But wouldn't he have been caught when she was rescued? She had no way of knowing.

A plan began to resolve itself in her head. Tomorrow they could go down to Bloomington and use the Indiana University library. If she had been kidnapped, there would be a report in the newspapers. The trouble was, she didn't even know the year, much less the month. Or even her last name. She scrapped that plan.

Maybe the best thing would be to call the Marshal's Office in LA and find out what kind of records they had. They probably wouldn't tell her on the phone, however.

She needed some action to relieve this anxiety, this crippled feeling in her mind. She was an adult, not a helpless child.

CHAPTER SIX

He decided to watch Blythe Kensington's television exposé on his phone again. Maybe something would come to him.

She was good. Almost as good as her partner, van Pelt. Now *there* was a wise guy if he had ever seen one.

It clicked in his mind then. *Partner. Van Pelt.*

Maybe they were more than partners. Maybe they were a couple. It was worth a try.

* * *

In the morning, he had Norris look up the utility records in Cook County for David van Pelt. He struck gold. Van Pelt lived in Winnetka right on Sheridan Road. Dressing in a white overall and bringing the ubiquitous clipboard with him, he drove to Winnetka.

He could afford to live in Winnetka, but he preferred the country. Unless he was working, he lived at Lake Geneva. When he was in town, he had a condo on the Gold Coast. The drive to van Pelt's home took only half an hour with the traffic all going into the city.

Mr. van Pelt's home was a white brick Georgian with black shutters and trim. He could find no evidence of an alarm which was criminally stupid on the news man's part. It was a piece of cake to put on his latex gloves and let himself in the service entrance in the back.

Then he began his search. First, bedroom. No women's clothes or toiletries. Blythe Kensington was not living here unless it was in one of the other bedrooms. When he looked, however, there was no trace of her.

As long as he was here, he would do a thorough job. It wasn't like he had any other leads.

He went downstairs to the office. No computer. He must carry a laptop. File cabinets. He toiled over them for half an hour. Nothing pertinent to Blythe Kensington. Desk. Likewise nothing.

He was beginning to think he had wasted his time here when he went into the kitchen. There, right next to the range, was the charging station for van Pelt's phone. And it was sitting there, plugged in.

Could it be that simple? Why would the guy leave his phone?

Because he was using a burner. The newsman knew about GPS chips and tracking, of course. So, he must want to be somewhere off the grid.

He placed a call to WOOT and asked to be connected to van Pelt.

"Mr. van Pelt is not in the office," a chipper assistant said.

"Is there a number where I can reach him?" he asked.

"What is this regarding, sir?"

He hung up. He would bet his Lamborghini the man was out of town with Blythe Kensington. Had they gone to California in the wake of the marshal's death? Would they find some records on the Kensington case archived somewhere?

Before he had the cop, Norris, check the airlines, he went through news man's telephone. The last call made on it was to another area code. On a whim, he redialed.

"Brick Street Inn," a cultured voice answered.

"I'm sorry, I must have dialed the wrong number," he said. "What area code is this?"

"Indianapolis, sir."

Bingo.

He hung up.

CHAPTER SEVEN

David woke with a feeling of unease. It took him a moment to identify the cause. *Smoke. The smell of gasoline. Outside his door.*

Alarm jangled his mind fully awake. The smoke was beginning to make him cough. Grabbing his cell phone, he called 911 and reported a fire at the Brick Street Inn, simultaneously wrapping himself in blankets and stumbling into the suite's living area.

"Fire!" he yelled. "Fire!"

He tripped into Paula's room and found the door to the hall ablaze. Almost unconscious, she was coughing up smoke.

Cursing his wound, he dragged her from her bed with all the strength he had. Through the window, he could make out a crude, iron fire escape. Fortunately, Paula didn't weigh much. Putting her down for a moment, he threw up the double hung window. Then, cradling her in his arms, he straddled the sill.

His wound broke open, and blood seeped through his t-shirt, the pain intense. But fresh air began to revive Paula; she coughed and wheezed.

"Honey, can you stand on the fire escape? I can't pull us both through."

"Oh my gosh, David! You're bleeding!"

She managed to get herself out, still coughing and sat on the fire escape. David heard sirens. Using all his remaining strength, he managed to finish stepping over the sill. The fire raged behind him in Paula's room.

A bullet whizzed by his head. "Gunshots! Get down!"

They both fell, coughing, onto the old metal structure of the fire escape. Another shot fired. David heard the claxon of the fire truck.

They couldn't descend the stairs while someone was shooting at them, but flames were licking out the window now. They were sitting ducks for the gunman and fodder for the fire. His heart was pumping blood out of his chest with every beat. His body covering Paula's, David passed out.

* * *

Paula felt David go completely limp on top of her. "David! David, hold on. They're here."

She began screaming to the EMT's below. "Help! Up here! Man critical!"

Soon the emergency workers were swarming the fire escape. Paula was still coughing. The fire was now at her back climbing up the outside of the building. The first worker reached her.

"Take him first. The blood is spurting through his chest. He had surgery last week. Blood vessels. Lung. Please save him!"

The EMT cradled David carefully in his arms and walked awkwardly down the fire escape. Paula followed slowly, her left arm hanging awkwardly and hurting like the devil.

"I've been shot," she said to the EMT who met her on the ground.

Though the EMT was a female worker, she hoisted Paula into her arms and took her to a waiting ambulance. They were laying David down on the stretcher, and an EMT was staunching the arterial flow from his chest wound with a huge white bandage. It was soon drenched with blood. Another EMT was inserting an IV into his arm.

Guilt clamped down on Paula's heart as she coughed. She should never have let him come away with her. What if he should die because of his chivalry? Longing to throw herself on top of him and stop the blood with her body, she began keening, "Oh dear Lord, save him, save him. Please don't let him die. Oh, Lord . . ."

"Here, now," said the EMT working on David's wound. "You have to calm yourself."

"It won't do anybody any good if you get hysterical," said the female worker. "Now you need to put this oxygen mask on."

* * *

Barely controlled chaos reigned in the ER of the Kindred Hospital North. Paula was wheeled through the entrance on a stretcher. David went before her. She couldn't see his face, but an IV pole containing saline rolled along next to him, and an EMT was running along with his stretcher applying pressure to his chest.

"We have to take him straight into surgery, ma'am," the female EMT told her gently.

"And you need to be treated for smoke inhalation and a bullet wound. After that, the police will need to get a statement from you. Don't worry. He's in the best of hands. This is a good hospital."

The hospital nurses took over from that point.

"Thank you," Paula murmured to the EMT's retreating back. Tears leaked from her eyes.

God, please. Let David live. This is all my fault. He doesn't deserve to die.

"I'm just going to give you a local anesthetic while we clean this wound. We're going to keep that oxygen mask on you for a while. I'm going to run an IV because you need to hydrate. You've lost some blood."

The words went in one ear and out the other. She lay like a limp rag while they poked and prodded. Apparently, they got the bullet out of her arm and stitched up the wound.

While they were bandaging it, an enormous police officer made his way into her cubicle.

"She can't talk yet, Lieutenant," said the nurse. "Her blood oxygen level is too low. She needs that mask for a bit."

"I'll be back," he said. "Are you admitting her?"

"No. But from what I understand, her husband is upstairs in surgery. She'll probably want to go up there to wait on him."

"I need to talk to her first. Don't discharge her until I do," he instructed.

* * *

The large policeman's name was Lieutenant Simmons. Paula was sitting in the surgery waiting room when he found her. She had just finished giving her information to the admitting desk, and as much of David's as she knew.

"According to the fire chief, this fire started outside your bedroom door."

"Is that beautiful inn a total loss?" she asked.

"Your . . . Husband called 911 right away. We were able to save the ground floor, but there's water damage."

"I don't know how they found me, but the arsonist and shooter were after me."

"Tell me," the lieutenant said.

"It's kind of a long story, and I don't know most of it."

Paula explained about her parents' deaths, her own juvenile traumatic amnesia, and how she had found out she was in WITSEC.

"Wait," the lieutenant said. "You're that reporter that broke the story about that mob boss down in Arkansas?"

"Yeah. David, the man in surgery, is my partner at the news station. He was wounded in the chest. He hadn't healed yet, but the marshal who put me in WITSEC was killed in Chicago, so I thought I'd better go into hiding. David came with me. We're trying to find out what the situation was that put me in WITSEC and why they're after me. Why the marshal was killed. The only clue we have is that whatever happened to me happened in the Orange County area."

She told the lieutenant the little she knew from Marshal Sutherland's daughter, spewing it out like the poison that it was. The insane situation might have killed David.

"How did this person know you had come to Indianapolis?" the lieutenant asked.

"I have no idea." She went through all the precautions they had taken. "Obviously he's an evil genius. We're not dealing with amateurs here."

"It's just a guess," he said. "But it looks like you're up against some pretty sophisticated organized crime. That marshal moved fast to get to you, but it wasn't fast enough. You moved fast to get out of Chicago, but it wasn't fast enough."

"And now they might not be able to save David," she said, hanging her head.

"I'm going to put in a call to the U.S. Marshal's Office in Orange County and bring them up to speed on what's happening here. I'll see what the best way is for you to get the real story of what's going on. Something huge must be at stake, I'm guessing."

Yes. Something huge. It didn't end when we went into WITSEC. It's been growing all this time.

"You get upstairs to your partner. When I've talked to the marshal's office, I'll come and find you."

Whatever wooziness Paula still felt from her ordeal was pushed to the back burner when she began her vigil in the surgery waiting room. She was not alone. There was a weeping mother or wife sitting trying to read a magazine. A distraught man paced, pausing only now and then to look out the window.

Paula didn't know what to do with herself while she waited. It occurred to her then that she and David had just lost both their computers and all their clothes. She didn't even have a phone.

How had the killer found them? What was so urgent that necessitated her being killed? Had he followed them to the hospital? What were they going to do now?

Linking her hands in her lap, Paula closed her eyes and tried praying but her thoughts were too scattered. All she could manage was "help me," and "save David."

She was very glad when the lieutenant appeared.

"Your name is Blythe Kensington," he said. "Does that sound familiar?"

A name. Finally, her last name! "Not at all."

"I found a place where we can have a little privacy. It's an office down on the first floor. Can you come with me?"

"I don't want to leave here in case the doctor comes out."

"It will only take a few minutes. I didn't find out much."

She followed the lieutenant down the stairs onto the first floor and into a small office that was cluttered with charts and books and papers.

"An admin's office. She's out today," he explained.

"All right. What did you find out?"

"Well, no one in the Marshal's Office was really familiar with the case, since it happened so long ago. They just knew from Marshal Sutherland that his trip dealt with Blythe Kensington, a WITSEC case from years ago. The marshal checked out all the paper files they still had and took them with him when he went to Chicago. They, I assume, were taken by his murderer when he killed Sutherland."

"That's what I figured," she said with a sigh. "Don't they have computer records somewhere? The case wasn't *that* long ago. Around the turn of the century, I figure."

"There are computer files, but they are on an external hard drive which is stored off-site in a place they didn't specify. They are going to send some FBI agents to us out of Orange County. They need to question you about the marshal's death and this incident." Because there was only one chair, the lieutenant's large frame hovered over her. He continued, "They are going to try to get the computerized case files before they come. I would expect that they are indexed somewhere. They won't share them with you, however, until they know you are who you say you are. They'll take your fingerprints, which are on file."

Paula bit her lip. "My instinct at this point is to take poor David to the Outer Hebrides and sheer sheep for a living."

"Outer Hebrides?"

"Islands off Scotland. Very scarcely populated."

He gave a little half smile. "That would probably be safe, but your David might get a tad bored. Instead, I think you ought to allow the FBI to help you. There is no reason this should all be on you. They will be here tomorrow."

She couldn't look past the next few hours. "We'll just have to see how the surgery goes."

"Your assailant is just waiting for you to leave the hospital so that he can try again. He may even try to come into the hospital." The lieutenant ran a hand through his curly black hair, clearly uneasy. "I've spoken to the administration. They are cooperating."

The policeman was going above and beyond his duty for her. She needed to show a little gratitude. "Thank you, Lieutenant."

"Mr. van Pelt will be put in a room with an extra bed for you. I'll have one of my sergeants guarding your door. When the FBI comes tomorrow, I'll bring them to you."

"I don't even know if David is going to make it," she said.

The lieutenant put a kindly hand on her shoulder. "I'll wait with you 'til we get news of the surgery's outcome. Have you had anything to eat today?"

"No. I don't want anything."

"You need to keep up your strength. You need it to heal yourself. I'll meet you upstairs in the waiting room after I raid the vending machines."

Paula went back upstairs to the weeping mother/wife and the pacing man. Everything the policeman told her paled in the wake of her worry for David. She would worry about everything else when she found out if David survived his surgery. This was the second time in two weeks she'd had to face the reality that he might die.

It had probably been selfish of her, but Paula had been glad when David's engagement had ended. During their last investigation, they'd been thrown together in life-threatening positions, and though he was still engaged, he'd given her reasons to think that he cared about her. Had it just been an impulsive feeling driven by their situation? Since the marshal had called, they'd scarcely had a chance to take a breath. With a heavy heart, she wished she had never led him into this dangerous mess.

The police lieutenant appeared with an anemic looking ham sandwich and chips from the vending machine, along with bottled water.

"Thank you again. I don't even have any money to pay you. Everything was burned up in the fire."

"Put that out of your mind for now. Suppose we wile away the time, by your telling me the story of how you took down Magnus O'Toole," he said. "That was quite a feat."

Sighing, Paula did as he asked without much enthusiasm. She even managed to eat the sandwich and chips. She drank all the water.

At last, a doctor emerged and said, "Anyone here for David van Pelt?"

"Here!" she said, getting up as he walked towards her.

"Mr. van Pelt should do well. He lost a lot of blood. But I managed to put some stints in place and repair the rest of the damage. He needs to rest. How long has it been since his last surgery?"

Relief washed over her in a warm wave. "About ten days. The problem is someone is trying pretty hard to kill us."

"Well, he's going to be in the hospital at least a couple of days."

The lieutenant stepped up. "I told Ms. James that I'll arrange for a police sergeant outside their door."

"Is he awake yet?" Paula asked the surgeon.

"He's getting there. You can sit with him in recovery. A nurse will come in a minute and take you back."

"Thank you for your fine work, doctor." She turned to the lieutenant. "Are you coming with the FBI tomorrow?"

"Yes. I want to coordinate with them to try to put away this arsonist."

"Thank you so much for everything you're doing. I don't know what I would have done without you today. I'm so relieved David is going to be all right."

He patted her on the shoulder and turned to leave.

* * *

The first thing Paula noticed was how pale David was. His skin resembled parchment. There were charcoal circles under his eyes. She longed for him to wake up, so she could talk to him and reassure herself that he had come through the surgery all right.

She took his hand and began to stroke it in circles with her thumb. Who knew life as an investigative journalist could be so dangerous? Who knew being Paula James, or should she say Blythe Kensington, could be so dangerous?

Finally, he opened his eyes and looked around. "Paula?" he croaked.

Her heart sped up. "I'm here, David. Thank the Lord you're alive."

"What happened?"

"There was a fire. You carried me out the window and ripped open your wound. An artery began to spurt."

"Is that a bandage on your arm?"

"Yeah. There were gunshots, too."

David brow lowered. "Are you okay? How bad is it?"

"They removed the bullet and stitched me up. I'm also on an antibiotic. I'm going to be fine."

"I'm glad. Sorry I was such a wimp. How the devil did they find us?"

"That's the question of the hour." She wanted so badly to put her head down on his wounded chest and hold him close. Instead, she squeezed his hand. "You're lucky to be alive."

"So are you," he scolded. "I don't like this, Paula."

She needed a diversion. "The nice lieutenant who is handling this found out my name for me. Blythe Kensington."

"Nice lieutenant, eh? How'd he do that?"

"He called the District Headquarters in Orange County, California, where Marshal Sutherland worked. They knew my name. That he was coming to see me."

David looked at her, seeing past her light façade. "You know that whoever is behind this attempt on our lives must have a devil of a good reason. You know something that is putting him in danger *now*." Pausing, he looked up at the ceiling, his brow furrowed in thought. "If this is still concerning what your father and/or your mother testified about, there is something about that case, whatever it was, that's still unfinished. Someone who isn't in prison."

Paula thought about this. "If he'd gotten all the bad guys, we wouldn't have had to go into WITSEC."

"Right. And there is no statute of limitations on kidnapping. If you were kidnapped, and I think that's what makes the most sense, particularly after what Janice Sutherland said, the person behind the murder of Sutherland and the attack on us was probably concerned in that. He probably knows you can identify him."

Chills raced down her arms. "He doesn't know I've lost my memory."

"So you won't know even if you're in his presence. That's a huge danger, sweets. I think it's really important that you see a hypnotist, maybe a therapist who does hypnotism, as soon as possible."

Paula thought about this. "Maybe there's one who works with the FBI in Orange County."

"I don't think you should go to Orange County until we know more than we do. It would be like stepping into a hive of killer bees."

"The lieutenant said that they would not release the WITSEC file to me until they are satisfied with my identity—oh, but you don't know—agents from the FBI are coming here. Tomorrow."

"Good." He looked up at his IV. "I won't be much help, I'm afraid."

His face seemed to have gone a shade paler.

"David, you just got out of surgery. Don't concern yourself with this right now. I almost lost you. Your life is more important than anything."

"I don't know what in the world they put in those IVs, but I need to kiss you, he said."

She brought the hand she held up to her lips and, with all the devotion she was feeling, kissed it. Then he brought their clasped hands to his lips and kissed hers.

A nurse came in and pulled back the curtain surrounding his bed. "Looks like you're ready to go up to your room. Let me check your vitals one more time."

"They're putting a bed for me in your room, and a policeman at our door," said Paula. "I'll follow you up."

CHAPTER EIGHT

On his phone, he found a place to buy scrubs. After purchasing a package of greens, a white lab coat, and one of the shower-cap things surgeons wore, he checked into a hotel and had some lunch. He was banking on the fact that since both of his targets had been carried off by ambulance, they would be in the hospital for a while.

After lunch, he changed into the scrubs and put the cap in his pocket. In his other pocket, he carried his Glock and a suppressor. He would go in during the four o'clock shift change when things were at their most hectic. Sitting back on a stack of pillows on his bed, he used the remote to find ESPN and watched some golf.

CHAPTER NINE

Sergeant Weber had heard all about the people he was guarding. They were modern-day legends—investigative journalists who had taken down a drug lord who proved to be a notorious crime boss long believed dead. Usually, he didn't favor the media much, but these guys had been working among the most hated of all— dirty cops.

So, Weber wanted to make sure Mr. van Pelt and Ms. James were safe. He knew the man after them was of another most-hated group, a man who'd killed a U.S. Marshal. He wasn't going to get past Sergeant Weber.

Because of this, when the man in a lab coat and scrubs appeared not to notice him and pushed his way through the door of room 405, he was not intimidated.

"Doctor, I need to see your ID."

The man kept going. Weber leaped out of his chair and pulled him back by his well-muscled arm. The sergeant held on as the man struggled to get out of his grasp. They were inside the door to the room.

"I'll have your badge for this!" the man said, just like someone on TV.

"I don't think so," said Weber.

Using his other hand, the man fumbled in his pocket and pulled out an automatic with a silencer. He aimed it at van Pelt. Pure instinct prompted Weber to drop the man's arm and karate chop his wrist, causing him to drop his weapon.

With an ugly sneer, the man whirled around and aimed a blow the policeman's jaw. Weber dodged out of range, slipped behind the guy, and put him in a chokehold. He used deadly force, keeping his captive turned away towards the hall. He increased his hold until the man went limp. As the sergeant went for his cuffs, the guy came to life, squirming out of Weber's loosened hold and sprinting down the hall.

The sergeant took off after the man, chasing him into a stairwell. They both clattered down to the second floor, where the perp ran out onto Surgery. The hall was empty except for a nurse wheeling a cart with glass tubes of blood. Seizing the cart from her, his prey pushed it right towards Weber. He dodged, and the cart slammed into the wall. The splinter of glass sounded as he resumed the chase, chagrined that the man had gained enough distance to go through the emergency exit. Alarms clanged through the hospital.

When Weber got through the door, he was just in time to see the perp jump from the outdoor staircase and roll to his feet. Raising his weapon, Weber aimed, but the runner was dodging back and forth through the cars and ambulances pulled up to the ER.

Weber ran down the staircase, but by the time he reached the bottom, his prey was no longer in sight. Cursing, he picked up the radio on his belt, called off the fire engines and reported his failure to capture.

CHAPTER TEN

A struggle between the sergeant and a man in doctor's scrubs in the doorway woke Paula. Confused at first, she saw the "doctor" aim an automatic with a silencer at David who was still sleeping.

The threat immediately crystalized. This was the man who wanted them dead. Her impressions of him were just a blur as the fight moved out into the hall. He was short with a hooked nose. A surgeon's "shower cap" covered his head, but his face showed black stubble. She got out of bed and was just in time to see the sergeant run out the door that she assumed led to the stairwell.

Her heart was galloping like a racehorse. If Lieutenant Simmons hadn't put the sergeant on their door, both she and David would be dead right now. Was there ever going to be a place where they would be safe?

Sitting in the chair between their beds, she pulled up her legs and hugged her knees. Paula looked over at David. He had slept through everything.

The sergeant came back in. "He got away, but I got a good look at him. I'm calling the precinct for them to send over a sketch artist."

Paula's voice was hoarse as she said, "His gun is still on the floor. I assume that's a silencer on it?"

"It is. He was a very nasty customer. Had you ever seen him before?"

"No. I think he must be a hired killer. A clever one, too. Somehow he traced us here to Indianapolis." She shivered, not changing her position in the chair. "Thank you so much for saving us." Her shivers morphed into trembling.

"Let me put in that call. I'll be outside the door."

David had awakened at the sound of their voices. Paula told him what had occurred.

"This guy just won't give up," he said.

"Sergeant Weber is getting a sketch artist in here. We both saw him pretty well. They can put out a BOLO on him, here and in Chicago. I'll bet someone knows who he is."

"We can get the sketch on WOOT news," David said.

"I am almost positive he is only a cog, though," she said wearily. "The people who are after me will get someone else if he goes down."

"Chin up, sweets. The FBI is coming tomorrow.

* * *

Dinner was tired-looking roast beef, mashed potatoes, and gravy. After they had eaten, a slim young woman with her strawberry blonde hair in a ponytail arrived along with the Sergeant's relief. The new policeman was Sergeant Duncan. While Sergeant Weber briefed him, Paula worked with the sketch artist.

"I'm Penny," the young woman she said as she set up her portable easel. "We'll just start with general things. What shape was his face?"

"Long. Boney," said Paula. "He had scruff. Dark, black scruff."

"Nose?"

"It was hooked. It might have been broken across the bridge at some time."

She sketched in the nose. "Longer," said Paula. "And there was a bit of a bump on the bridge where it went crooked." Penny's pencil flew. "Yes. You've got it."

"Eyes?"

"I'm afraid I didn't get a good enough look. I only saw his profile."

Sergeant Weber entered and looked at the sketch. "Good start. The guy's eyes were little and close together. He had almost no lashes. Like a lizard."

Penny worked fast.

"A little more round," Weber said.

"Did he have well-defined cheekbones?"

"Yes," Weber and Paula chorused.

"They were high," Paula said. "Right under his eyes."

"And the skin sort of hung from them," said the Sergeant. "Slackish."

Sometime during this process, Paula had stopped trembling and had put her feet down on the floor.

"Sounds like he's someone I wouldn't care to meet," said David.

"Now," said Penny. "Mouth."

"Fleshy," said the sergeant. "Bow-shaped, like a woman's."

"Small or wide?"

"Small. And his nostrils flared a bit more," said Weber.

They went from there to the forehead, chin, and ears. The sketch that emerged was amazingly like the man she had seen. "That's incredible, Penny. I think people should be able to identify him from that."

"I'll go make copies at the station and then they can take it into the local TV stations for the eleven o'clock news and the morning shows."

A little red-haired nurse came in to check David's dressings and vitals, give him his nighttime meds and test his blood oxygen level. All were doing well. She tested Paula's blood oxygen level while she was there.

"You could probably use some more oxygen," she said. "I'll see to it."

When she brought in the oxygen and put the cannula in her nose, Paula tried to breathe deeply and relax. So much had happened in such a short time, her poor brain and psyche were overwhelmed.

"I don't know if I am ready for the FBI, David," she said.

"Are you afraid you'll have another panic attack?"

"Yes. Everything is happening so fast and furiously. And I don't even have Petey."

"So what am I? Chopped liver?"

She smiled. "As I told you once before, you don't fit in my bag."

"We'll talk to the FBI here in my hospital room. Tell them that we work together and that's the only way you will do it."

"I'm a woman. I'm supposed to be able to handle these things."

"Paula, I don't mean to talk down to you, but in matters like we're dealing with now, you're still a traumatized child. That child is buried deep inside you. And I wouldn't be at all surprised if she has PTSD."

She thought about this. "You know, I never thought of that, but I'm sure you're right."

"Good. I'll remind you in the future that there was one time when you said I was right."

Paula took the cannula out of her nose and walked over to his bedside. "Hospitals are murder on romance," she said, looking down at him with his cannula, his IVs, and a silly hospital gown. "But I'm so glad you're alive, you look great to me."

He gripped her hand. "I think we've got to learn to live in the moment, Paula. If we think of everything we've got to sort through, it can become overwhelming."

"Agreed," she said. "And even though it's pretty noisy in this place, I think we ought to try to sleep tonight. We're going to need it."

* * *

The FBI agents arrived after breakfast. They looked far from intimidating, Paula was glad to note.

Special Agent Forrest was only about 5'8," with blond hair and a seriously receding hairline. However, his eyes had laser-like focus and were chips of lapis in his tanned face. Special Agent Moreno was slightly taller, but whip-cord thin with enough energy emanating from him to light the room. Probably nearing fifty, he was obviously Hispanic though his eyes were clear green.

"You two look like you've seen better days," said Agent Moreno.

"Not lately," said Paula. "With everything that's happened, it seems like David has had that wound forever. Did you, by any chance, hear about our last story?"

"Yes," said Agent Forrest. "Impressive."

"Were you able to bring my WITSEC file?" asked Paula.

"Yes," said Agent Moreno. "Although before we can reveal the details, we need to verify your identity." He opened up an IPad, and after a few moments, handed it to her and had her place her fingertips in the designated spots.

"It'll take a few moments to put these through IAFIS," he said, typing out the request on the keyboard.

"In the meantime," said Agent Forrest, taking out his phone, we can begin your account of the situation with Marshal Sutherland."

The agent recorded on his phone her account of her conversation with the marshal. She told him how she had gone to the meeting place the next day and the marshal had not shown.

David then said, "You may not be aware of this, but Paula has juvenile traumatic amnesia. She remembers nothing before she was ten years old and living in Lawrence County, Missouri. She never knew she was in WITSEC until the FBI told her there was a flag on her file during our last case."

"No. We didn't know that," said Agent Moreno. "That means everything we have to tell you will be news, right?" he asked Paula.

"Yes," said Paula. "And I am assuming it is going to be unwelcome news."

"Yes. Probably. But you need to know it, so you can figure out why you are in someone's crosshairs at the moment." He stopped as his IPad beeped. "Okay. We have a match. You are Blythe Kensington."

"She never even knew her name until yesterday when Lieutenant Simmons obtained it from the Marshal's Office," David said. "You have to realize that the things you are going to tell her about her past could very well be traumatic for her since she has suppressed them."

He looked at Paula. She was glad that David was informing them of the way things stood, but it made her a bit self-conscious.

"I think you should show them the scars, Paula," David said.

"That won't be necessary. We have an account of them in the file," said Agent Forrest. "I think we should get on with the interview now." He pressed the record button again. "Tell us why you decided to leave Chicago and describe the events that took place when you arrived in Indianapolis."

Paula tried to compose herself by taking a deep breath. It felt as though smoke lingered in her lungs, and she coughed. "We decided that since the murderer of Marshal Sutherland knew he was coming to Chicago, that he was probably killed to prevent him from telling me why I was in WITSEC and all the details surrounding it. We understand the files he brought—my WITSEC files—were taken when he was murdered," said Paula. "The criminal probably hired the killer when he saw me on WOOT TV. I understand I looked just like my mother when she was younger. But I have no idea how he found out about the marshal coming unless he has an informant." She paused. "We picked Indianapolis at random, and no one knew where we were going. Not even WOOT. We have no idea how he traced us here. We rented a car under an alias."

"Did you bring your phones?" ask Agent Moreno.

"No," said Paula.

"Where are they?" he asked.

"I have no idea," she said, looking at David. "Our admins picked them up from us at a meeting point. I assume they took them to the station."

"Geez," said David. "What if they took them to our houses? They had the keys. And the last call I made was to make reservations at the Brick Street Inn in Indianapolis."

"We're dealing with a pro here," said Agent Forrest. "He would have been sure to break into your house."

"But how did he even know I was accompanying Paula?"

"He had some luck there," admitted Forrest. "But that's how he must have traced you."

"David woke up to the smell of smoke. He had to carry me out, and that's what reopened his wound."

"Tell me about this wound," said Agent Moreno.

Paula said, "Magnus O'Toole shot him in the chest about ten days ago. David nearly died. And he nearly died this time, too."

"The dude still didn't give up," said David. "He targeted us here in the hospital yesterday, but Lieutenant Simmons had the foresight to put the excellent Sergeant Weber on our door. He saved both of us. Guy had an automatic with a silencer."

"What happened to it?" asked Agent Moreno.

"The sergeant took it away with him," said David.

"We worked with a sketch artist last night," Paula said. "We ended up with a pretty good likeness."

"What did you say the Lieutenant's name was?" asked Agent Forrest. "I'll give him a call. Indianapolis PD has facial recognition software, I'm sure."

"Simmons," Paula said. "His card says Zionsville PD."

"I'll call right now," he said, stepping out of the room.

Paula felt a sense of relief. These guys were wasting no time.

Agent Moreno said, "This is all very troubling that they would be so determined to silence you after all these years. You must know something pretty damning to someone."

"That's what we figure," said David.

Agent Forrest reentered the room. "The sketch went down to IPD this morning. I put a call into them to speed things up."

"Okay," said Paula, squaring her shoulders. "It's time for you to tell me the big secret."

Agent Moreno turned off the recording.

"Did you know your father used to be a cop?" he asked.

Considering that her father had spent his last days cooking meth, the news was a shock. "No," she said.

"He worked vice, and he was one of the best undercover operatives in the business," Moreno continued.

Another shock.

"He was so good; he took down an entire operation. It reached from Mexico clear up to Seattle on the north and Nevada on the east."

"My father did that?" asked Paula.

"Yes. He was incredibly brave and incredibly good. Marshal Sutherland put your whole family into protective custody to keep you safe, so your father could testify in court."

"But something terrible went wrong," Paula said in a small voice.

"Yes. They had a dirty cop they didn't know about. Somehow, he figured out where your safe house was. It was attacked. There were guards there, and they protected your parents, but they failed in your case. You were kidnapped."

Paula's heart fell, and her hands began to shake. So she and David had been right. Suddenly she wanted to tell them to stop. The fragile box that held her feeling of security was collapsing around her.

"At some point, we are speculating that you were thrown from the car, and that is how you broke your arm and leg. You were so traumatized when you were rescued that you didn't speak. When you finally recovered your speech, your memories were locked inside your head." He paused, his green eyes turning softer with compassion. "I am sorry to tell you this, but the kidnappers never treated your injuries. You had a broken arm and leg, as well as severe cuts and contusions on your left arm and leg. You were only wearing a nightgown. That must be why you were so badly scarred. It's an absolute miracle you weren't killed.

"You were in captivity for a month before we finally rescued you," Agent Moreno's voice was heavy. "I can't tell you how sorry I am for what you went through then. I was on the team that found you. You had been starved and beaten. Videos were taken and sent to your parents. Your father said he wouldn't testify until we found you."

Paula felt the room recede and her mind shut off. The fizziness began on the top of her head. She tried to drag herself to her bed but stumbled and fell to the floor. Her whole body went catatonic. She could only stare and hear; she couldn't move.

"Did you have to go into such detail?" David cried out. "She's having a panic attack for crying out loud. I can't get out of my bed with these blasted IVs. Pick her up. Bring her to me. Lay her beside me!"

Paula felt one of the men take her up under her arms. The other took her feet. They laid her beside David in a small space he had made. He held her close with his good arm.

He whispered in her ear. "Darling, darling Paula. I'm here and I'm not leaving you. Anyone who is after you will have to go through me. You are strong. You are not that little girl. All that happened to someone else."

Agent Moreno pulled up a chair up beside the bed. "Your father was an incredibly brave man," he said. "I knew him. The takedown, your kidnapping, and the trial took their toll. Afterward, all he wanted was to get away from the evil and raise you in a little farm community. That's why the Marshal moved him so far away. But in the end, it drove him crazy. He got in touch with me right before he died. Did you know that he was working his own undercover project then? But, he told you, didn't he? That's why you went after O'Toole."

Paula heard the words, but her mind shunned them. It couldn't process anything more now. She was in her dark place. And she didn't want to come out. If she did, something horrible would happen.

CHAPTER ELEVEN

David didn't know what to do. Stroking Paula's hair, he listened to the words Moreno was saying. At the end of his recital, David was astonished. Paula, if she could focus, would be so relieved at the knowledge about her father.

But all the information Moreno had given them had troubled him badly. Not only was it unbearable to think of Paula suffering so much as an innocent child, but there was obviously a present-day threat. The trial was long over. Someone powerful enough to hire a killer didn't want Paula alive. Something she had seen back then threatened him. And now that someone knew Paula James was the grown-up Blythe Kensington.

Could she handle all this horror? He was certainly having a problem with it. Especially when lying prone in a hospital bed.

One of the agents' phone rang. Forrest moved out into the hall to take it. He was back within minutes.

"We have ID on the man who's been after you. Billy Porter. He's a hired killer out of Chicago. Wanted for several murders. Word on the street is that he costs a bundle. Now that he knows you've seen him, he will be especially anxious to put you away. Is there anywhere safe you can go? We can see that you get there."

"I'm not getting released from here for at least another day," said David. His mind went back to the almost idyllic days he and Paula had spent in Grand Rapids when they had gone off the grid during the last investigation.

Paula needed more help than he could give her. How could anyone process the information she had been given? He stroked her arm, but she was still unresponsive.

Where is the best place to take her for treatment?

He knew what his father would tell him. Mason Clinic in Minnesota. A doctor in rural Minnesota, in his father's opinion, Mason was the best at everything.

"Could I borrow your phone?" he asked Forrest. "I need to check something."

Forrest looked startled, but then handed it over. David dialed his dad's number. It was Saturday, so he would be at home.

"Dad? It's David."

"Good to hear your voice. Are you involved in another harum scarum case? That last one was quite a doozy. How're you feeling?"

"I'm recovering well, thanks. Hey, I have a question for you. Remember meeting Paula James at the hospital in Arkansas?"

"Yeah. Your partner, right?"

"Yes. Well, she suffers from juvenile traumatic amnesia, and apparently what she doesn't remember is putting her in danger. We need to retrieve those memories, but they're bound to be pretty traumatic. Just the bare bones of what happened are horrific, and she is having a difficult time. I was wondering about the Mason Clinic. Do they have a psychiatric unit?"

"They do. It has a really good reputation. You want me to do some checking for you? See if they can treat this sort of thing?"

"That would be great, Dad. You can call me back at this number. The sooner the better."

Paula began to stir. "No," she said. "No."

After returning the agent's phone, he held her close.

"We will leave you for a bit," Agent Moreno said." "We'll be down in the cafeteria, setting up a BOLO on Billy Porter. He has to be staying around here somewhere."

When the FBI had gone, David asked, "How do you feel now? Do you want to sleep it off? I can still hold you."

"Yeah," she drawled. "It's still passing off." That said, she immediately closed her eyes and drifted off.

He thought about her panic attacks. It seemed to him, after watching her, and thinking of the other he had witnessed, that they were motivated by fear as much as anger. Perhaps it was a combination of the two. She was angry, but bad things had happened to her when she had shown her anger, so she suppressed it. Her nervous system became overtaxed and shut down. Paula needed this out of her life. How could she cope otherwise?

He held her so close he could feel the beat of her heart. David could not imagine a little girl having so much violence inflicted on her—unattended injuries from being thrown from a car, starvation, beatings. No wonder she had suppressed the memories. It was a wonder she had survived at all.

He had never been the violent type, but he wanted to murder these people if they were still alive. He wondered if she would be able to bear the return of those memories. Was it too much to ask of her?

How could he, with all his self-consequence and flaws, ever be enough for her? He hadn't been enough for Sherrie, and she was self-sufficiency personified.

But had he really loved Sherrie? She had been aware of his phobia about commitment. She had actually been the one to pop the question. And hadn't it been him and not her who was waffling about the wedding date? They hadn't come close to setting one.

He tightened his good arm around Paula. *Blythe.* How could he ever be enough for her?

Soon exhaustion overcame him, and he slept beside her.

He peered out from behind the curtain where he was hiding. Mom would take away his TV privileges if she knew he was still awake. He tried to calm his breathing. She had the hearing and awareness of a bat. Bats were freaky. So was his mom sometimes. He swore she could read his thoughts.

There was that man again. He always came in after the babysitter left, and it was always on nights when Dad was at the hospital. Why did he kiss his mom like that? It was like he was trying to eat her. And they didn't talk. They just kissed. Finally, they left the room, and David heard them climb the stairs. When he heard the bedroom door close, David darted out of his hiding place and scampered up the stairs, keeping to the edges so they wouldn't creak.

He was jerked awake and disoriented by the trundle of the lunch cart. Ugh. Rice and meatballs, cottage cheese with pineapple. Jello with Cool Whip for dessert.

"Wake up, sweets. It's your favorite. Red jello!"

She stirred.

* * *

After lunch, they had some good news from the agents who paid them another visit.

"They caught Billy Porter in a traffic stop as he headed out of town," Moreno told them. "We can't pin the marshal's murder on him, yet, but we got him for assault and attempted murder. We've got his gun, and in Chicago, they will have the slug that killed Sutherland. Hopefully, we'll get him for the arson, too.

Moreno's eyes were shining, and David could tell it was a great day for him when they got a killer of this caliber off the streets.

"Ms. James, will you be able to pick him out of a line-up later today?" the agent asked.

"Yes," she said.

"Sergeant Weber will do the same. There are a lot of arrest warrants out for this guy."

Forrest added, "But we're keeping the arrest on the down low now. We don't want the people who hired him to know he's out of commission. You're safe for the next little bit, anyway."

"Thanks, guys," said David. "We haven't done much deciding about where we want to go. We've been sleeping."

"Sleep's good. I got a call on my phone from your dad," said Forrest. "He wants you to call him back." He handed his phone over.

Paula had moved over to the chair to eat her lunch, so David raised his bed and dialed his dad.

"Hi, Dad."

"Hey, David. I checked out the Mason psychiatric clinic for you. They don't have anyone in-house who does hypnosis, but they have a good therapist who works on people who suffer from juvenile traumatic amnesia. There is a hypnotist they sometimes work with if it becomes necessary."

"Thanks, Dad. It sounds like just the ticket. I appreciate your help."

"Let me know if you need me to make arrangements. You'll need a referral. I liked Paula, especially because she saved your life."

"Will do."

He decided to wait until the agents had left again before trying to convince Paula to go to the Mason Clinic. Instead, he said, "Marshal Sutherland has a daughter, Janice. She may know some more details now that she has had a chance to think about things. She got in touch with Paula by phone when she came to Chicago after her father's murder. We were already down here in Indiana, so we didn't get a chance to see her."

"Thanks," said Forrest, writing the name down in his notebook.

"Not much else we can tell you right now," David said.

"You can let us know when the line-up is ready," said Paula.

"We will. Are you going to feel up to it?" asked Moreno. "That was some episode you had. Was it epilepsy or something?"

"No," Paula said, and David knew she was reluctant to discuss it. "I'm fine now. I suppose you will interrogate that guy about who hired him?"

"Yes. And hopefully, he'll talk in exchange for a lighter sentence. We'll leave now and go down to the Indianapolis PD to meet the fellow." He wrote down the address on his paper tablet and ripped out the page, handing it to Paula. "There's the place you need to go."

"I don't have a driver's license, an available car, or money for a taxi," she said. "We lost everything in the fire."

"We'll send a squad car for you, then."

After they had left, David watched as Paula pushed the nurse call button, and then requested a comb, a toothbrush and toothpaste. "I would love to take a shower," she said to the nurse whose name was Alicia. "I still smell like the fire."

"You'll have to keep the bullet wound dry, but I'll find you some shampoo, if you can manage washing your hair with one hand. And I should be able to find some clothes if you don't mind wearing scrubs."

"Anything else rather than my Wonder Woman pajamas."

When the nurse had left, David laughed. "I didn't even notice we're both in our nightwear. I'm glad I was wearing sweats."

"You'd look very Cary Grant in pajamas," she said with a vestige of her normal humor.

CHAPTER TWELVE

Paula was ready when the squad car came for her. The policeman looked somewhat askance at her in her green scrubs, but she ignored him. At least her hair and body were clean. Alicia had redressed her wound with a fresh bandage, and she wished she could say she felt as good as new.

Paula guessed she would probably never get over the idea that she had been kidnapped; she was only glad she still had no memory. She hoped she never would.

The idea of going through "memory recovery" terrified her. She knew enough about her fragile mental health to know that if she submitted to such an experiment, she might never get over it. There was a reason her memories of those awful traumas were locked away inside her mind.

But maybe that was the only route she could take to find the main monster—the man who wanted to eradicate her forever. Someone her father hadn't even known when he testified. Her mind rejected that choice. Surely, they would offer some kind of deal to this assassin if he would divulge the name of the man who had hired him.

The Indianapolis Police Headquarters came up all too soon. She was not looking forward to seeing the man who had nearly burnt her and David to death, who had shot her and then tried to murder them in the hospital room. What would the eyes of such a man look like?

They took her to a room with a large window set into the otherwise colorless wall.

"Just sit there, and in a moment, a parade of men will come in and stand looking through that window. All they will see is a mirror," said a uniformed policewoman.

"That is the man I saw in my hospital room," Paula said

"And what did you see him doing?"

"He was dressed like a doctor, but he was aiming an automatic with a silencer at my partner, David van Pelt when he was sleeping in his hospital bed. Then Sergeant Weber karate chopped his wrist, and he dropped the gun. They began to fight, but he got away. I never saw him again until now."

"Thank you, Ms. James."

She was led out of the room, and the policeman who had driven her, escorted her back outside to his squad car. Without speaking, he opened the back door for her. They made their drive back to the hospital in silence.

She was very glad to be delivered back to her sanctuary in David's hospital room.

"How are you feeling?" she asked him. He was sitting up watching CNN.

"Everything is starting to itch. Did you ID the man?"

"Yes. It was horrible. Let's talk about something else."

"My Dad called. He said Mason Clinic would be a great place for you to go to do the memory retrieval thing. They have a good psych department."

Everything in her rose up in stubborn rebellion. "I've been thinking. What if this man, this Billy Porter I identified will agree to a deal where he will divulge the name of the man who hired him? The idea of trying to recover those memories scares me to death. I don't want to do it unless there's no other way."

David's eyes softened in contrition. "I'm sorry, Paula. I guess I've been so focused on getting to the truth of this threat that I haven't really thought about what it would mean for you. You seem so strong. But obviously you were helpless when those things happened to you."

"I don't know how you can think I am strong when I am constantly melting into a puddle of goo."

"Your body is protecting itself. You know, now that I think about it, I'm not at all sure this is the way to go. As you said, this man may agree to a deal. Let's not make any plans just yet."

Paula sank onto her bed, feeling a surge of relief at the reprieve.

"Mr. Q called while you were gone. He's Fed Exing another credit card, so we'll have cash. But, neither of us has a driver's license. Maybe we should go back to Chicago and get our licenses renewed before we do anything else."

She went to the window and looked out. A spring storm had blown up. Thunder echoed through the room. "It won't be long before the man who is behind all this hires someone else. I think we should stay out of Chicago for the time being. We only have to go into Illinois to get our driver's licenses replaced."

"You're right, of course. I want to think the threat is over, but you're not safe as long as that psychopath thinks you know who he is."

Paula began trembling and rubbed her hands up and down her arms.

"Come here," David said.

The gentle tone of his voice melted her icy fears. Going to his side, she sat on the edge of the bed. He sat up and took her into his arms. For a moment he just held her close. Why did the nearness of this particular human being seem to make all calm inside her? Her heart quieted, and her shaking ceased. The past could not be undone, but for the moment it receded to a safe distance.

"I'm not Superman, but I will be beside you through this, Wonder Woman."

She blushed. "You noticed my pajamas."

"I couldn't exactly help it."

"Just get better, okay? So we can leave this place. I don't exactly have warm and fuzzy feelings about Indianapolis."

He gripped the handle with the call button. "I'm seeing if Alicia will give me the okay to go for a walk."

"You don't have clothes, silly!"

"They must have a bathrobe or something."

He was right. They did have a thin cotton robe that he was able to put on so they could go for a walk outside in the hospital gardens as soon as the rain ceased. In the meantime, they settled for the cafeteria where they both had hot chocolate while the thunderstorm blew itself out.

They did not talk about the situation. Instead, they spoke of their hopes and dreams—the station David hoped to own someday. Steering away from anything personal, Paula did not speak of her desire to have a family eventually. She could not think of anyone she would rather stand with through thick and thin than David, but she didn't know his feelings. Finally, they were able to go out the patio doors into the warm, humid air. Summer was definitely on its way.

She had no money, no clothes, no phone, no ID, but at least David was doing better, and Billy Porter was in jail. She still had her life.

Later, after they had lunch, the FBI returned.

"He's not talking," Agent Moreno said. "I imagine that if he talks, he'll be killed in prison, and he knows it. Whoever his boss is, he's so powerful that he could make that happen.

"He'll be tried in Federal court. Capital punishment is possible in the murder of a Federal Marshal if the forensic evidence from Porter's gun matches the bullet used to kill Sutherland."

"His 'boss,' whoever he is must be one powerful man."

Agent Forrest asked them, "Have you decided what you're going to do when you get out of here?"

She was still not ready to consent to go into the Mason clinic. "How long will it take them to process the forensic evidence in Illinois?" she asked.

"They'll probably do it immediately, so he can be extradited there to face the more serious charge of murder of a Federal Marshall for hire," said Agent Moreno. "I'm taking his gun with me up to Chicago so that they can match the ammunition."

Paula had noted that Agent Moreno was a lot more talkative than Agent Forrest who stood with his back to them looking out the window.

"So. Have you decided what you're going to do now?" asked Agent Forrest again.

Paula didn't see how it was any of his business. She exchanged a glance with David and gave a minimal shake of the head. "No. We just want David to get better so we can leave the hospital. I think he needs a nap right now."

"We'll go then," said the Latino agent.

When they had left, David turned to her, eyebrows raised. "You're having trouble trusting law enforcement; I take it."

"Yeah. I am. They don't need to know where we're going."

"Did you hear any of what they said during your panic attack?"

"Yes, I heard it all. But it was like it bounced off a steel wall. I don't remember it."

"Agent Moreno said your father was working undercover before he was killed. He decided on his own to take the Arkansas organization down. He was in touch with Moreno. You ought to talk to him about it."

"So he didn't go bad. He wasn't cooking meth for the money!" Heavy care loosened inside Paula and floated away. "I always rationalized what he'd done by saying he was doing it for my mother, but that means a lot to me to know he wasn't bent at the end of his life. And he didn't tell me, because he didn't want me to go after the guys myself if he got killed. Remember that note he left me?"

"Yeah," said David. "He told you not to trust anyone and not to try and go after anyone. He knew you took after him."

"So, he trusted Moreno," she said. "He knew the FBI in Bentonville was dirty, so he didn't trust anyone around the area, but he still trusted Moreno clear out in California."

"Yes. And Moreno rescued you when you were kidnapped. I think you can trust him, too."

"Okay. But if I do this memory retrieval thing, I still don't want anyone to know about it. Including Moreno. He might tell someone. I'll be a target for sure if anyone finds out."

"Agreed. But the more I think about it," said David, "the more I don't want you to have to go through that."

"Now that we know Porter won't talk, it's the only way I can see that we have a chance of ending this thing," Paula said. "We need more information, and with the Marshal dead this is the only way to get it."

* * *

The following morning, before breakfast, David's doctor did his rounds. He pronounced David's wound to be healed enough for him to leave the hospital, but cautioned him strongly, "You are not in any shape to be skirmishing with criminals."

As the nurses were doing their final check-ups, a FedEx package arrived containing the new credit card.

"Never will I be this happy again to go shopping!" he said.

"You aren't going anywhere in that bathrobe," said Paula. "I am only slightly better in my scrubs, but I think I'm at least fit for Walmart. I'll take a taxi there and get us some clothes to get started with. Then, once you're dressed, we'll go to the Fashion Mall everyone has been telling me about and make a day of it. We both need some happy time."

They carried out this program to the letter. Fashion Mall was a fun place. They ate at a western-style steakhouse where it was acceptable to wear Walmart jeans. Paula shopped for not only clothes but make-up and bath gel. David was happy to let Paula choose his clothes, but at the end of the day, he was exhausted.

"Let's find a plain old Fairfield Inn and spend the night," she said. "No drama. Then tomorrow we'll have to take the bus into Illinois to get our driver's licenses."

They were tucked up in their separate rooms when they watched the ten o'clock news. The lead story dealt them a stunning blow.

"In a bloody battle at the Indianapolis City Jail, alleged killer-for-hire Billy Porter has escaped. Evidence suggests that he had help from the outside. Viewers are asked to contact the police if they recognize this man."

His booking photo was shown. Paula gave a little cry and doubled over. David swore.

Paula felt panic invade her body with such a mighty shock that she ran to the bathroom and vomited. David hammered on the door.

"This room has two beds," he said. "I'm sleeping in one of them."

"I don't think I can sleep," she said.

"There's no way he can know where we are," he told her. "But I know it's going to be rough for you tonight. Let me stay."

"All right," she said. "Do you think you could just hold me?"

"It's the least I can do for Wonder Woman. Between us, we've got this dude."

CHAPTER THIRTEEN

David lay awake long into the night, while, contrary to her expectations, Paula slept soundly. Lying next to her while they both stood in such peril spurred him to self-examination.

He was making all kinds of promises to Paula. Promises to stand by her, not to let her down, to be there for her. All his adult life he had been wary of such promises. Now it seemed they were coming out of his mouth every time Paula faced another crisis.

David knew from his association with her through grad school, and after that, she had never been the needy sort. In fact, she had always held herself a little apart from people. Now he knew why. Unlike others, she didn't have a life experience of relationships to draw on.

She had not opened her heart to anyone since her childhood. David suspected that there had been a time when she had openly and freely loved other people, but since the kidnapping, she doubtless thought that people you were close to could abandon you. Wouldn't that be the way a child would see kidnapping? As a betrayal?

She had always struck him as someone who lived in the present moment. Now he knew that that was the only way she *could* live. She didn't have a past of loving and being loved. Paula was afraid to trust.

So was he. While Paula's parents hadn't actually betrayed her, his mother *had* betrayed him.

His mind shunned the painful experience. Would he ever be truly able to commit to anyone? Would he be able to keep the promises he made to Paula to stand by her?

* * *

The bus ride to Danville, Illinois was a fairly short one. All in all, it took less time than the bureaucrats did at the DMV.

Paula had decided to renew her license as Ellen Templeton, the alias she had used on the last case. It was the one that was in the computer. Because of the fire, she had no other ID. Fortunately, the pictures the DMV personnel brought up on their old licenses matched their faces well enough that they were finally issued the new IDs.

Next, they rented a car. They sat in the Chevy Impala, rented under the name of Ellen Templeton, looking at one another. "Where now?" said David.

It pained him to watch the struggle on Paula's face. "I guess the next step has to be the Mason Clinic," she said. "I think we're out of other options."

"Are you sure, sweets?"

"No. But do you have any other ideas?"

David thought that there had to be a very good reason why a villain from her life seventeen years ago was now so afraid of being identified. Was he currently set up as an ordinary guy with a whole new life to lose? Or was he simply so drenched in crime that ordering murder was the way he solved any problem? Someone had sure gone to a lot of trouble to get Porter sprung from jail.

"We're dealing with someone extremely dangerous," he said. "This has to be your decision. I don't have any other ideas."

"All right." She handed him the burner phone she had purchased for him the day before at Walmart. "Call your dad. See if he can get us into the Mason."

He pressed in the well-known number of his dad's office. His secretary put him right through.

"David, how are you doing, son?"

"Well. But my friend, Paula, has decided she needs to go ahead with the memory retrieval process. It's urgent. Could you see if you could use your pull to get us admitted?"

"I'll sure try. Is Paula certain that this is what she wants?"

"She's got a steel will, Dad. She doesn't see any other way to find out what's going on in our lives."

"She must be brave. You take good care of her, y'hear?"

"I intend to."

"Okay. I'll make the call."

Without anything else much to do while they waited, they went to a drive-thru burger place.

"This looks like it has the exact thing that I want."

"What's that?"

"A huge chocolate shake made from scratch."

"Coming right up."

His dad called back just as he and Paula finished their shakes.

"You're in first thing tomorrow morning. Show up on the fourth floor of Building C. They want to do a preliminary physical—just the basics. Then you go to the psych wing."

"Okay. Thanks a million, Dad."

"Are you ready to fly to Rochester, Minnesota?" David asked Paula.

"Not from Danville. Let's drive to O'Hare and go from there. It's not that far."

* * *

During the drive to O'Hare, Paula was mostly quiet. When she did speak up, she said, "Your dad seems like a good guy. I've never heard you talk about your family."

"My dad *is* my family. He is a great guy. He loves his work, but I think he had something else in mind when he went to med school."

"He's a doctor in a small town, right?"

"Yeah. I'm sure he chose that path because he thought it would be the best thing for me. If he had followed his inclination, he probably would have gone into clinical research at Johns Hopkins. He's a brilliant man."

David could feel Paula's puzzlement. "In what way would a small town be better for you?"

"He needed someplace family friendly since he was a single dad. I don't think he liked the idea of me growing up by myself for long hours in Baltimore."

"That's quite a sacrifice. He must love you a lot. But what happened to your mom?"

"She took off during his residency. In her defense, it must have been a brutal life. He did his residency at the Mason Clinic. The hours were awful. He always says that she just decided she didn't sign up to be a single parent. So she started over with someone else. She lives in Minneapolis now. She's principal of a grade school. Her husband is a high school science teacher. They have three kids."

"I'm sorry," she said. "How awful for you."

"Yeah, well. Dad and I are close. He gave me a good life. And he's supportive of my career."

He thought for a few minutes. "You know, looking at things in perspective, I think Sherrie probably thought I was going to be a workaholic like my dad was when he was a resident. Maybe she made the right decision for both of us."

Paula said, "You love your job. That's for sure. A woman would have to understand that."

"Yeah." He decided to change the subject. "You'll like the Mason Clinic, I think. My dad took me on tours sometimes. The total of all the brain power in that place blows me away."

CHAPTER FOURTEEN

The campus of the world-famous Mason Clinic was daunting, but the people there proved to be kinder than anyone Paula had ever met.

"Welcome to the Mason," said the nurse who took her vitals. "Is this your first visit?"

"Yes," said Paula. "I'm a little nervous."

"It shows in your BP, but that's not unusual. Your pulse rate is up, too. Do you mind if I check this bandage? What happened?"

"It's a long story, but I was wounded by a bullet."

The nurse seemed to take this in stride. "Well, it looks like your wound is healing well. I'll replace the bandage, and then I'm going to put you on a straight water IV. You're a little dehydrated."

"Can my partner join me while I'm getting it?" Paula asked.

"Of course."

The cheerful nurse called David in after she had set up the IV.

"How are you feeling?" he asked.

"Nervous. Really nervous. The nurse thinks I'm dehydrated."

"So. You're really going to do this thing," he said. His eyes grew intense with the cherishing look she loved so much. "You know, I admire you more than anyone I've ever known. This willingness to go back to a time when you were so victimized is nothing short of heroic."

His words warmed her. She certainly didn't feel heroic. More like a scared child. She *really* did not want to do this. "I just hope it yields something helpful."

* * *

The psych building was very soothing in appearance. The walls were a warm rose hue and were hung with friendly flower paintings. She only had a short wait in a reception area furnished in putty-colored leather.

Though she hadn't asked permission, she brought David through with her. She had decided that heroic or not; she wasn't willing to make this journey alone.

Dr. Adams, her therapist, was a classy looking woman in a cocoa-colored pantsuit with a cream-colored blouse. She looked to be in her forties, which comforted Paula for some reason. Her blonde hair was in a bun on top of her head, and she wore squarish glasses with red frames. Her office was paneled blonde oak with a large window overlooking a pond with ducks.

"Welcome to the clinic," she said, shaking hands. "You are Paula James, and this is?"

"My partner, David van Pelt. He is here to keep me grounded. He knows my story as well as I do, which isn't much."

"Why don't you tell me what you hope to achieve from our sessions? I have information on your intake sheet, of course, but I would like to hear it from you."

Paula looked down and pleated the fabric of the gauze skirt she wore. "I don't remember anything from before I was ten years old living in Missouri." She paused and just decided to jump in. Looking up, she met the therapist's eyes and said, "In just the past several days, I have learned a little bit about that time. According to the FBI agent I spoke with, I was in witness protection or WITSEC. The things that happened to me before that time were extremely traumatic—a kidnapping, a car accident from which I received some injuries, as well as physical abuse. I think the reason I can't remember is that my brain is shutting down those memories so that I can function in the present."

Paula paused to wet her lips. *This is all so out there. I sound like some weirdo.*

"There is someone out there who wants me dead because of what he thinks I remember. So I need to find out *what* it is so I can find out *who* he is." She appealed to the therapist, "I have heard that therapy and hypnosis can help retrieve lost memories."

David intervened here. "Excuse me for interrupting, but it's pretty important that you understand that Paula has barely survived two attempts on her life this past week."

"Attempts on her life? Good heavens. Suppose you start by telling me about those, Paula." Dr. Adams looked pointedly at David's sling. "I see that you have been hurt, too."

Paula explained what had happened in Indianapolis.

"I thank you both for helping me to understand. I must tell you though that I think you are expecting too much out of this process. We don't find hypnosis a reliable tool for retrieving memories. Just as often as not, you make false memories that way, which I am sure you realize can be very dangerous for your mental health and sense of identity." The doctor leaned forward in her earnestness. "We use the hypnosis strictly as a tool to help you relax. We rely on therapy to try to restore the memories that you are blocking. It's not like you can just take a pill and all the memories suddenly reappear."

Paula felt a mix of relief and disappointment. "That is slightly less scary than what I was expecting."

"It could still be painful. I suggest that we have a session of one hour twice a day for a week. We should know by that time if it's going to work. Do you have a place to stay?"

"No. Not yet."

"Would you like to be admitted as an inpatient?"

"I don't think so. I would like David to be able to sit in on the sessions."

Dr. Adams looked at David. "That is very unusual. Are you certain?"

"Yes. He's my backup in case things get crazy. I'm prone to a rare form of panic attack where I become catatonic. David knows how to deal with them. It makes me feel safe to have him here."

The therapist looked from one of them to the other. "That's your prerogative." Returning to her desk, she wrote something down. "Here is a voucher for a room in our outpatient living facility."

Paula cleared her throat and said, "Would it be possible for us to have two rooms?"

The therapist looked taken aback. "Why yes, I suppose so." She handed Paula the vouchers.

"Now, let's get started. I have asked Mrs. Mae Lawrence to start today with a little hypnotic exercise to relax you a bit. You have nothing to fear from her or what she will do."

She pressed the intercom and invited Mrs. Lawrence to enter. The woman proved to be very petite with red hair and freckles. Paula realized she had been expecting someone who looked a bit gypsy-ish, and almost laughed at herself.

After they were introduced, she asked Paula to move to a reclining chair in the corner of the office. They then dimmed the lights.

Paula fidgeted in the chair. Soon there was the sound of waves on the beach with the occasional cry of a seagull. Then Mrs. Lawrence began to speak very softly telling her to tighten and release her different muscle groups, starting with her toes, and working up to her head. As Paula complied, her body began to feel heavy.

When Mrs. Lawrence had completed this part of the program, she bade Paula to think of a place where she had been contented and to picture herself there. Paula envisioned sitting on the shore of Lake Michigan in Evanston. David was at her side. They were simply sitting, talking about school, planning their futures.

She felt completely calm and started to drift off to sleep. Then Mrs. Lawrence told her she was going to count to ten and Paula was to emerge slowly from her drowsy state to being completely awake. She would be able to think clearly and carefully consider the questions Dr. Adams would ask her.

The hypnotist counted to ten and raised the chair. Paula felt calm and comfortable. Mrs. Lawrence slipped out of the room, and Dr. Adams turned up the lights.

"Are you ready to answer some questions, Paula?"

"Yes," she said.

"What is your earliest memory?"

"Playing with Barbies at the beach."

"Who was with you?"

"Janice."

"How did you feel?"

"My arm and my leg were hurting. I had casts on them."

"Was anyone else there?"

"Janice's father. He was sitting a little ways away from us. Looking worried."

Paula felt wrung out. She sagged in the chair. "I can't believe I remembered that. It must have been because I recently talked to Janice. She called me when her father was killed."

"The father that was at the beach?"

"Yes. He was the U.S. Marshal assigned to protect my family. About ten days ago, he was coming to tell me everything about my being in WITSEC. He said I needed to know for my safety now that my parents were dead. You see, they hadn't told me anything. I only found out from the FBI during our last investigation. Anyway, the marshal was shot in the head before we could meet. My file was taken."

"I think we had better back up. Why were you in WITSEC?"

Paula answered, telling her about her father's job and his role in taking down the drug operation. "I was kidnapped to try to force my father not to testify, but fortunately I was rescued by the FBI."

"You have been through so much, Paula. My brain is whirling. You are a very strong person to have survived all of this. No wonder you have psychogenic memory problems."

"Psychogenic?"

"Memory problems caused by trauma." The therapist smiled at her. "I think this is more than enough for today. It was a success. You brought up a memory."

* * *

David put an arm around her as they left the clinic and went to their rental car. "You had that poor woman almost speechless. Will she be able to help you do you think?"

"I hope so. It wasn't as bad as I thought it was going to be. And I did pull up that one memory. I like her. I like that she's clinical. It makes things easier."

They reached their rented Focus, and Paula pulled out the map of the Mason Clinic's campus. She gave David directions to a block of cocoa colored apartments.

"They look nice," she said.

David agreed. She noticed him looking around the staircase as they climbed to their rooms.

"What's wrong?" she asked.

"No security cameras. I hope they have decent locks on the doors."

"You are afraid someone is going to find us *here*?"

"Our pet killer is at large again, remember?"

"But we left without telling anyone! No one knows where we are."

"Forrest and Moreno know. They overheard my phone call with my father."

"You don't trust the FBI?"

"I don't know who to trust, sweets. We've got to be very careful."

As she unlocked the door to her apartment, Paula shivered with a wave of anxiety.

He said nothing while she examined her new living space. It was a small studio, painted yellow with a sage green carpet and pictures of poppies on the walls. The galley kitchen had a counter with stools. A list of local food delivery services sat on the counter. The bed pulled out from the couch, and there was a flat-screen TV and a recliner.

"Why don't you see what kind of food you want while I unpack?" she said. "I'm starved."

Later, after David had unpacked in his apartment, they sat at Paula's counter and ate pizza and an order of cole slaw. Paula was suddenly exhausted, and they opted for an early night.

"How is your chest?" she asked, as they parted at the door.

"Healing." Leaning down, he gave her a gentle kiss.

Paula was overcome suddenly with the need to be close to him. She entwined her arms around his neck and kissed him more deeply. "Thank you," she said, laying her head gently over his wound. "Thank you for being here for me. I will never be able to repay you. I'm so closed off, David."

"You don't have to repay me, sweets. I know you are tied up in knots. I want to be here. And you know, we're working on a heck of a good story."

She looked up at him, and he grinned.

"Right. Like my psychoanalysis is going to be breaking news."

"There is a big liar at the bottom of this tangle, sweets. We're going to find him. We're that good."

"We are good," she said and kissed him again.

As she lay on her hide-a-bed that night, Paula tried to think of where the relationship with David was headed, but she couldn't see beyond the present moment. Almost dying and knowing she was still a target made it extremely difficult to see beyond the necessity of survival. And if she was going to survive, she had to make a success of this therapy business. She was very glad that she had David at her side to weather the experience with her. She realized it wasn't the right time to try to figure out if what she felt was love or an unhealthy dependency that he would tire of and eventually find too difficult.

* * *

After her relaxation session with Mrs. Lawrence the following day, Dr. Adams said, "Tell me about your arm, Paula."

In response to this question, a clear picture of her lovely mother formed in her mind. Until recently, Monica James had always been tall and elegant. Paula focused her thoughts on earlier times.

"My mother wouldn't leave my side until they wheeled me into surgery. And when I came back to consciousness in the recovery room, she was right by my gurney. She smoothed my hair with her hand and kissed my cheek." Paula felt tears form in her eyes which surprised her. Tears didn't come easily to her.

"Go on," said Dr. Adams, handing her a box of tissues.

"She explained to me that they had had to break my arm again to set it properly. My leg, too. She said there would be pain, but that I would be fine when I had had some physical therapy."

"Did she say anything about the scars?"

Paula felt the tears streaming down her face now at the memory of her mother's anguished face. "She told me skin grafts would be painful, but if I wanted to have a pretty arm and leg again that I would have to have more surgery. I begged her just to let them be. I didn't like them putting me to sleep. I was afraid that when I woke up she wouldn't be there.

"She just died at the beginning of March. I haven't mourned her until now."

"How did she die?" asked Dr. Adams.

"Bone cancer," said Paula, weeping hard. "She just wasted away. In the end, she left me, just like I always knew she would."

"Do you think that was her choice?" asked Dr. Adams.

Paula bit her lower lip, tears still falling. She blew her nose. "I do think she was tired of life, but I pretended to be strong, so she didn't know how much I minded her going. She was in a lot of pain. I didn't understand then about her aversion to pain drugs. I didn't know my father had been undercover in a drug organization for years. I didn't know that his testimony brought down a huge operation. I didn't know the enormous price my mother and I had paid to make that happen. So many things . . . "

"And what price was that?"

Paula began to feel agitated. The window into the recent past faded away. She was once again firmly in the present. "I didn't know about how he was undercover and then the kidnapping. I can't imagine how hard that must have been on my mother."

"Very good, Paula. Excellent. You have made real progress in accessing your feelings about your mother's death." Her voice was gentle and soothing.

Paula could not stop her weeping.

"You are not that little girl any longer," Dr. Adams said. "You are crying for her. You are feeling abandoned as you felt when you were kidnapped. There are layers of feelings here you have never expressed. We have to get down below everything you have been suppressing if you want to find the things you want to know. But I must warn you; your mind might never let you go there. This process will take a huge toll. I think we should call it a day and forego our session this afternoon."

Paula blew her nose again. Her heart was heavy with grief. She just wanted to go someplace to cry it out. Someplace safe. The pond outside the doctor's window with the ducks beckoned to her.

David helped her to her feet and they both thanked the doctor as they left.

"I'm going to take a walk, David. Why don't you go back to the apartment and have a nap?"

"I know you are processing some heavy stuff, Paula. And I know you don't like me to see you cry, but you need me by you. For safety's sake, first of all. But also because I can't bear to leave you alone. You've suffered enough abandonment."

His unexpected response enveloped her like a warm cocoon, but she said, "I need to get these feelings out. It's unusual enough for me to cry, but to cry in front of you is even more difficult. Please trust me in this."

"All right. Where will you go?" His frown of concern was almost her undoing.

"To the duck pond."

"How about if I pick you up in a couple of hours and we find something to eat?"

"Thanks. That would be good."

Pulling something out of his jeans pocket, he handed it to her. A blue bandana. "Handkerchief," he said. "Feel free to use it."

At the bottom of the stairs, he kissed her forehead and walked away. She wanted to call him back, but she knew this part of grief had to be suffered alone.

CHAPTER FIFTEEN

Billy Porter was extremely glad to be out of jail, but he still intended to go after his quarry. Excruciating memories of how they took him down kept visiting him. Billy Porter did not fail. And he certainly didn't go to jail.

Things were getting serious now. Apparently, his mark was undergoing some kind of treatment to get her memories of her captivity back. She was at the Mason Clinic. If anyone could help her, they could. His boss's exposure could come at any time. It was critical that he get to her before then.

Things were pretty hot for him. He was sure he was on the no-fly list. They had taken his false ID from him in jail, so they knew what name he was traveling under. He didn't have the time or the resources to obtain another one at the moment, so that meant he couldn't rent a car either. He had managed to get as far as Chicago on the bus. It stank.

Porter hated bus travel. There were plenty of cars on the police impound lot. His contact in Chicago PD had "arranged" one for him. Not the fanciest one he'd ever driven, but a Toyota Camry would be adequate and suitably anonymous. And no one would be looking for him.

He was on his way to Rochester.

CHAPTER SIXTEEN

David was antsy. The therapist might be pleased with Paula's progress, but he could see that it was going to be slow and agonizing. Her tears had smitten him. Now she was mourning her mother, and he couldn't imagine the pain she was in. He suspected these emotions had been with her in some form ever since the kidnapping. Had she suffered day after day during her kidnapping wondering why her parents didn't come to get her? All he could think of to do was to fold her into his arms and keep her safe from the past and the present.

His emotions were way out of control and probably wildly inappropriate. Being with her in her therapy sessions was forging an intimacy between them. Was it real? He didn't know what he was doing. He had gone way beyond his boundaries and most certainly had trespassed over Paula's.

When he found her by the pond, she was tranquil enough. But it was the kind of tranquility that came with great sorrow. He didn't know what to do.

"Another milkshake?" he suggested.

"Sounds good," she said.

As they drove to a Frostee's Drive In, she said, "You know one thing I'm glad of, is to know that my father was undercover during that year he was cooking meth. Even though he said he was doing it to pay for my mom's treatments, I lost respect for him. Now I have it back. Remember that letter he wrote to me that I found in my go bag?"

"Yeah. The one where he told you not to investigate?"

"Yeah. It makes more sense to me now. He probably wanted to tell me what he was doing but knew how dangerous it was. He knew about the sheriff, he knew about the crooked FBI agents, and he might even have known the identity of the guy behind the whole thing. But, he didn't know about you. He didn't know that I would have help and that together we could do it."

"And we did," said David.

She squared her shoulders. "And we are going to take the guy down that is after us, too. No matter what it takes."

"I'm afraid this whole process is way too hard on you."

"I haven't had real feelings for as long as I can remember, David. It feels good to grieve for my mother. As long as I was holding it back, there was a tightness in me that kept me from feeling anything but fear and anxiety. Maybe I won't have any more of those attacks. Maybe I'll just cry or get angry, or whatever a normal person does."

"I think that's a little too much to expect this soon," he said as they pulled into the drive-in. "But I think you're on the right track."

"This all must be terribly boring for you."

"Don't think that. It is a privilege that you will even think of taking me into this part of your life."

"I have been pretty inaccessible, but you need to know that your care and concern have meant more than you know. It is hard for me to feel safe. But for some reason, even just the sound of your voice has always made me feel safe."

Her words made him feel good, but way down underneath was some uneasiness. Would he let her down like he had let Sherrie down?

"Ready for your shake?" he asked too hastily.

Smiling, she said, "Definitely."

* * *

Dr. Adams was very solicitous of Paula the next morning. "How are you feeling?"

"I'm sad," answered Paula. "I miss my mother. But it is better than feeling hard as a stone."

"Are you ready to proceed?"

"Yes." Once again, David marveled at her courage.

She called in the hypnotist, who went through her relaxing ritual. When she was finished and had left the room, Dr. Adams said, "Tell me how you broke your arm and your leg."

David watched as Paula looked away from the therapist and bit her lip. For a while she said nothing as a faraway look appeared in her eyes.

"My mother used to sing to me," she said finally. "She would hold me on her lap and sing Negro spirituals. They were joyful songs, but there were some sad songs, too."

David heard her suddenly start to sing, "Going Home" with its universally haunting melody. Her voice was that of a little child.

It's not far, just close by
Through an open door
Work all done, care laid by
Going to fear no more.

58

Mother's there expecting me
Father's waiting, too
Lots of folk gathered there
All the friends I knew

When David choked up, he looked at Dr. Adams. She looked as though she was fighting tears. But, Paula just kept singing. When she was done, she went limp in her recliner.

David said, "I believe she's having one of her panic attacks."

Dr. Adams used a tissue to wipe her eyes. "She has regressed, shutting down the memory. How often does this happen?"

"It's happened a couple of times in the past weeks. She can hear us, but she can't respond. It's exhausting for her. She sleeps hours afterwards."

"Is this one of the things you help her with?"

"I have, yes. I don't know if it helps or not, but I usually hold her."

"Let's let her come out of it naturally, and see what happens," Dr. Adams said.

A burst of annoyance shook David. "She's not a lab rat! She could be like this for hours!"

Getting up, he went to Paula and stroked her cheek with the back of his hand. She was staring straight ahead, and her eyes didn't move. "I'm here. You're all right, Paula. You're safe. You've gone through the open door."

He took her hand and stooped beside her chair, ready to stay there, but Dr. Adams moved a chair beside him and he got up briefly to sit in it. He didn't let go of Paula's hand, but soothed it with his thumb. He could see that her jaw was tight, her teeth clenched.

The therapist spoke softly. "David's right, Paula. You're in a safe place."

But it was a very long half hour before she stirred, closing her eyes and then opening them to focus on David. "I'm sorry," she said, her voice slurred.

"It's not your fault," said David. "But I don't think you're going to be able to do this."

"I'm afraid I agree," said the doctor. "Whatever happened to you was so traumatic that you dissociated from it, your mind inserting another memory. Today you sang 'Going Home.' Do you remember that?"

"Yes. It was all that came. Besides that, there was just a wall."

"I don't know of any *good* way of breaching that wall," said Dr. Adams. "It's in place for a good reason. You are an extremely strong person to have successfully placed those memories where they can't reach into your conscious mind and destroy your peace. I also think that your mother must have been an extraordinary person to have helped you do that."

David watched tears spill over onto Paula's cheeks. "She was. She was amazing."

The doctor reached into a desk drawer and brought out a mini cassette. "I know these are out of date, technologically, but if you can find a little recorder that will play it, I think it will continue to help you. It is a recording of Mrs. Lawrence's relaxation technique. Should you have any trouble in the future, it could be helpful."

"So you're discharging me?" asked Paula, taking the little cassette.

"Yes. Our code of ethics here at the Mason Clinic is taken from the Hippocratic Oath: 'First, do no harm.' Anything further I may do would be harmful to you. You don't have these attacks very often, do you?"

"I used to when I was younger. My mother sang to me. But I've had several since we started this investigation."

"If after considering it, you still want to see if we can go back further and bring those memories you are masking out, we can work on it. But it will be a slow and a long process. And I certainly can't guarantee that knowing the details of what happened to you will set you free of those memories. I think your mother's way of teaching you to cope was a healthy response."

"We think that the person who did those things to me is still out there, that he is the one who is trying to have me killed," objected Paula.

"He is undoubtedly a psychopath or a sociopath. You will need more than a memory to put him out of business. I suggest that you continue your investigation using other methods."

David forced out the words, "We've done it before. We can do it again."

Paula raised the recliner and stood up. Immediately putting his arm around her, he said, "You gave it your best shot, and it almost scared me to death. We're done here."

She shook Dr. Adams's hand, and David did the same. "Thank you," they said at the same time.

"I will be watching the news," the doctor said as they left.

CHAPTER SEVENTEEN

The man known as Billy Porter arrived on the Mason Clinic Campus with no real clear idea of how he was going to find his target. The facility was huge and all protected by privacy laws. His contact in Chicago PD had given him a set of phony creds, but he guessed they weren't going to get him far.

At the guard station leading into the facility, he showed the badge which identified him as Roger Beeson, Police Lieutenant. He had applied a false tattoo to his neck above his collar. He knew this would call attention away from the details of his face. He also wore steel-rimmed glasses.

"We're investigating the death of the U.S. Marshal that occurred in Chicago recently. One of our material witnesses is here, receiving treatment, but I have an urgent need to question her. There have been other developments in the case. We are cooperating with Rochester, PD."

"I'm sorry, Lieutenant Beeson. I can only let patients and those they personally vouch for into the clinic grounds. I can't even verify that this woman you're looking for is here."

"But she may be in physical danger! Her life has already been threatened. There is reason to believe the killer may strike again!"

"Let me call my supervisor," the gatekeeper said. "Perhaps you could leave a note. I'll see."

Ten minutes later, a man who appeared to be the supervisor appeared. "What's the name of your captain?" he asked Porter. "He ought to know better than to send you to a medical facility."

Porter made up a name and endowed this fictional person with bulldog traits.

"If this person you are looking for is in danger, as my man has told me, you may write a statement to that effect, and we will use our own security to protect her."

It was all Porter could do to keep from taking the guy out with a well-placed punch. He took the pen and paper offered him and wrote:

Miss Paula James is in danger from the same contract killer that recently killed Marshall Southerland. He has failed once. We do not want her to go unguarded so that he can succeed next time.

As he stood in the gatekeeper's shed, he watched helplessly as a blue Focus carrying his quarry and her boyfriend drove through the gate and out of the compound.

Were they leaving for good? Or were they merely looking for something for dinner?

He cursed inwardly. Porter had no option but to follow through on his charade with the security guards.

After ten minutes that seemed much longer, the supervisor returned and said, "I am afraid we are not treating a Ms. Paula James."

He gave them the kind of look that they would not forget and left everyone standing as he returned to his Chevy.

CHAPTER EIGHTEEN

"Where now?" asked Paula when they were on the road to Minneapolis. "I feel like I've been cut loose from myself."

"Let's just find a nice hotel, have a good meal and then regroup."

"I'm so terribly tired," Paula said. "I think I'll skip the meal."

"We can have room service if you like."

"Sounds good to me."

When they checked into a Marriott near the airport, they took their few belongings inside, and David ordered Chinese since he had a craving for it. Paula didn't talk much as she picked at her dinner.

"You have just been through a meat grinder," he said. "Even Dr. Adams was shaken. Do you want to talk about it?"

"Maybe when I have some distance from it. Right now, I feel too vulnerable. I want to run away one minute then the next minute I just want to curl up with you and cry my eyes out."

"You're welcome to do either," he said smoothing the back of her hair.

"I think I'll settle for a hot shower and bed. Alone."

"This room has a pull-out couch for me. I'll be out here guarding the door."

She went to him and laid her head on his wounded chest. "You are the most patient man I've ever known."

"Only a loser would hit on you in these circumstances."

Taking his head between her hands, she kissed him with the little energy she had left. "Thanks."

After half an hour she was freshly showered and shampooed and lay in bed cuddling her pillow and missing Petey. The sounds of the airport were a white noise in the background, and her eyes drifted shut as she gave in to her exhaustion.

She was thrown about on the back seat as the car chased over the mountain switchbacks. It was pitch dark, and there was something in her mouth. It tasted nasty. The men in the front seat were silent. Suddenly the car twisted too fast, the driver applied the brake, and the back of the car started spinning taking everyone and everything with it. She was thrown hard against the door, and it opened. She hurled into the empty night.

Paula woke herself up screaming. In a moment, David barreled into the room and threw himself on top of her stiff and terrified form. "Paula! You're all right. You're here. It's all right. You're not a little girl. You're here in Minneapolis with me, David."

"I remembered," she said, her voice tight with fear. "About my arm. And leg. I was thrown out of a car going up the mountains really fast. I was sailing through the air. I must have landed in a ravine. Thank goodness I didn't remember that part. Just the falling and falling and falling."

"I'm sorry, Paula," he said, taking her in his arms. "I can't even imagine the fear you must have felt. And then, the pain."

She realized she was shaking. David was holding so tight the feeling of falling finally stilled.

"I didn't see anything. No faces. Nothing. I think I must have been blindfolded."

"That could be one reason you're afraid of the dark."

"I'm betting that I wasn't always blindfolded. Otherwise, no one would worry about what I saw."

"Obviously no one took you to a hospital."

"Something tells me they weren't into child care," she said. "You can ease up now. I know I'm not falling." He let go, and the space was back between them, but she immediately missed the feeling of safety he had given her.

She had always known, from the first time she had met him that it would be like that if he held her. Intense and safe.

"Your wound!" she said suddenly, pulling away further. "Oh my gosh. It must be killing you."

"It's all right. Don't worry."

"It was a really big car," she said. "Like a Cadillac or something."

"They must have held you someplace in the mountains," he said.

Another memory flitted quickly through her mind. "Wood. It was all wood. The floors, the walls. And there was a heater vent on the floor. It was burning hot."

"Sounds like an old-fashioned cabin someplace."

"That I would know again if I saw it. It was very different from my house, I think."

"Well, so far, none of this information is worth killing you over, but it shows you can remember. I'm not sure if that's a good or a bad thing."

"Good," she said. "That was not as bad as I thought it might be."

"You're amazing," he said.

"But, I'm not ready for you to go back to the couch. Could you hold me until I'm back asleep?"

"Of course."

* * *

The following morning when Paula awakened, David was asleep on the pull-out bed. She was swamped with love for him but didn't know if she should trust in it. Was she becoming dependent on him? *Definitely. Not a good thing.*

It felt like a good thing, but it really couldn't be, could it? Since she could remember, she'd always depended on herself. Everyone else always left her.

For a moment she sat and watched his face. It was gentle in repose, but she knew that underneath it was strong and determined. And definitely hard to resist.

He blinked his eyes open. "What's up?"

"Just admiring your jaw."

He put a hand up and rubbed it. "It needs shaving."

"I won't stop you," she said.

"What should I prepare for today?" he asked pulling himself up onto his elbows.

"Flying to California. I think we should follow Dr. Adam's advice and do what we do. We should have a look at the case documents. And I want to talk to Janice Sutherland in person."

"Sounds like a plan." Hoisting himself out of the hide-a-bed, he kissed her cheek and made for the shower.

CHAPTER NINETEEN

Billy Porter tried to put himself inside of Paula James's head. Why had she been released so soon from the Mason Clinic? Had they been successful already at restoring her memories?

As he cruised the interstate on the way to Minneapolis, he knew that such a thing would be disastrous. Why was she proving so hard to kill?

Supposing she had had her memories restored, what would she do? Where would she go?

California. She would go after his boss.

And that meant she would be flying to LA on the first flight she could book. It was just as well. She knew what Billy Porter looked like. He would subcontract his friend Gardner to take care of her and van Pelt as soon as they arrived in LA.

Just to cover all his bases, in case something went wrong with the Gardner plan, he needed to notify his boss that Paula James aka Blythe Kensington had her memory back and was on her way to California.

CHAPTER TWENTY

Arriving at LAX did not have the feeling of a homecoming. Paula still had no idea where her home had been. The crowds in the airport on this spring afternoon were so great that she decided it must be spring break for so many people to be traveling. She was bumped and pressed and sworn at.

Once they had the rental car, she and David had decided to stay near the beach, because something in her longed to be there.

"Let's go further south, this visit. Laguna Beach is supposed to be world famous. Let's go there."

They drove their rental car down to Laguna Beach where they splurged and spent WOOT's money on a tiny little bed and breakfast with room for only them. It was actually a studio apartment behind the owner's own home. The ad in the paper they had bought at the airport specified "Mature couples only. No students." Apparently, they qualified as a mature couple.

Their new residence was white stucco trimmed with mint green and white striped awnings. There were two hide-a-beds, functioning as mint green couches during the daytime, a marble table with fanciful wrought iron legs, a flat-screen TV, and the ubiquitous recliner. The kitchen was a tiny galley with miniature appliances.

"Before we unpack, or do another thing, we need to stretch our legs," said Paula. "Did you see that beach? It has tidepools!"

"What do you know about tidepools?"

"I know that I like them," she said thoughtfully. "Maybe the reason I wanted to come to this beach is that this is where I used to come with Janice."

They spent the afternoon exploring their surroundings—a winding cliff-top walk lined with palm trees and flower beds. There was even an English style bowling green where senior men in white clothing and hats played on the beautifully manicured lawn.

Next, they climbed the dramatic rock formations in search of tide pools. Paula was able to recognize several species of sea life and was so charmed; she nearly forgot the reason they were in Southern California.

Finally, they relaxed for milkshakes at the old hotel that joined the walkway to the Pacific Coast Highway. They took a break from discussing the case while they admired the fabulous view. Paula found herself relaxing completely under the influence of the rhythmic surf.

They walked back along the PCH, admiring the quirky little shops selling seashells and antiques. When they arrived at their little apartment, they decided they must start working.

Paula called her assistant, Liz, and got Janice Sutherland's phone number.

"How is Petey doing?" she asked.

"I am certain he is missing you, but he has taken to sleeping in my husband's slipper. He's adorable, and we love him to bits."

Paula had no sooner hung up the phone than she heard a huge explosion right outside her door. David had just come in with their suitcases and shut it.

She screamed involuntarily. David whipped out his phone and dialed 911. Paula and David looked out the front window of their studio and saw a tremendous fire right in the driveway. Flames were shooting what seemed like miles into the air. Their car!

The sirens started almost simultaneously and it seemed that the firemen were there in seconds.

Paula sat on the couch and trembled. Not again! Would they never be out of danger? If the explosion had happened just a matter of seconds earlier, it would have blown David to pieces. Her teeth chattered. She could not even speak.

He sat next to her on the couch, his arm around her as they listened to the commands of the fire chief over the blaze. Water hit the front of their studio right outside the door.

"That was a close one," David breathed. "But I don't think it will spread since they got here so quickly."

"I wonder if I'll ever feel safe again. How could whoever is after us have found us so quickly? We just arrived! We haven't even unpacked!"

"We must have been followed," David said, kneading the muscles on the back of her neck.

It seemed like an hour, but her watch showed only twenty minutes of peril before they had the fire out. There was a knock at the door.

"Fire chief," the knocker said. "It's safe to come out now."

David and Paula emerged hand in hand.

Behind the chief stood a policeman. He said, "Any idea why someone would want to bomb your car?"

"A hired killer is targeting us," David said. "It's a long story. You might want to confirm it with FBI Agent Moreno in Orange County, California. This isn't exactly the place to discuss it. Is there a coffee shop or something near here?"

"Up on the PCH and down a block is a diner called Joe's. We can get some coffee, and you can tell us your story there," said the fire chief.

"We'll go in my cruiser," said the policeman. "I'm Lieutenant Seager, by the way. This is Fire Captain Mendoza."

Paula said, "Paula James and this is David van Pelt. Thank you for getting here so promptly."

They climbed in the cruiser and took the short ride to Joe's.

The diner looked like it had been in its spot for a hundred years. It was definitely not fancy, which was fine with Paula. She felt like a dishrag.

Why did he blow up the car when there was no one in it?

An older woman in an old-fashioned, starched waitress's uniform seated them, and Mendoza said. "From the impact patterns, it looks like the explosion originated in the back seat. Passenger side," the fireman said.

Paula thought for a moment. "Oh my gosh! That's where I put my purse. But why would my purse explode?"

"When was the last time you were carrying it?" asked Seager.

"At the airport," she said.

"LAX or John Wayne?"

"LAX. We flew in from Minneapolis," David said. "The airport was very crowded. It would have been easy for someone to have slipped a bomb into her purse. It was one of that kind that is open across the top."

"Terrorists?" Paula asked. "Now we're being targeted by terrorists?"

"Probably meant to look that way. Could C4 have caused that explosion, Captain?" asked David.

"Very likely. Why?"

The waitress brought cups and poured coffee for each of them. She put creamer and sugar on the table. Paula poured half a pitcher of cream into hers and added several packages of sugar, all without thinking.

David began to tell their story. With each happening it seemed that it grew another volume.

"So you think this bomber is tied to someone who had you kidnapped in 2001?" the police lieutenant asked.

"Yes. The FBI thought they arrested everyone, but there must have been someone else because they put us WITSEC. Maybe they suspected they didn't get the main bad guy."

"Why would he be after you after all these years?"

"That's a really good question," Paula said. "I have no memory of that time. Psychogenic memory loss. I was only nine years old."

"And the Federal Marshal who was killed in Chicago was from here?"

"From the Southern California District."

"That covers Orange County," Seager said thoughtfully.

The fire captain spoke up. "I think the scenario probably went something like this: the airport was crowded, you say. Someone stuck a tracking chip and a small brick of C4 with a wireless receiver in your handbag. It wouldn't weight much. When they detonated it, they thought you were in the car, because the tracking device was in there."

Paula's hands flew to her mouth. "We could have been blown to bits at any time!" She began to shake again and couldn't stop.

"There must have been some divine intervention," said David. "Otherwise why did he wait so long to detonate it?"

Paula bit her lower lip, and he put his arm around her, holding her close to his side. "Were the press at the site?" he asked.

"Yeah. But we haven't given them a statement yet. They're sitting over there in the booth under the bad seascape," said the lieutenant.

"Do you think we could ask them to help us?" asked David. "Tell them to say that two unidentified bodies were found in the car? That would get this guy off our backs for a bit."

"We'd have to ask them to report misinformation," said Seager. "Their call."

"I'll go over and speak to them," David volunteered. "We're with the press, as well. This whole thing is our story. We're with WOOT TV in Chicago."

Paula watched him go over and sit at the booth with a man and a woman dressed in nice pants and tailored shirts. She hoped he gave them only the bare minimum of information.

The fire chief spoke, "You look like you could do with a vacation."

"Yeah. We both could. Whoever is after us doesn't give up. We have to keep going."

"Maybe the press will give you a break."

Apparently, David had enlisted their sympathy. "I promised them the whole scoop the same night that we go on air at WOOT. They've agreed to cooperate."

"Do you think we dare stay at that studio? It's so perfect," asked Paula.

"Our landlady may have issues with that."

"I'll speak to her," volunteered Seager. "She's well known in this area. She's been living in that house since the Depression, I think. Let's go there now. I think Ms. James needs to get where she can put her feet up."

CHAPTER TWENTY-ONE

"Seager must have charmed our hostess. I'm glad we don't have to move," David said.

He was worried about Paula. How much more could she take? Hopefully, this assassin would think he had succeeded this time and would leave them alone.

"Do you think you could eat some pizza?" he asked.

"No, thanks. But you go ahead."

He sat down on the other couch and leaned forward, his forearms on his thighs. "Look, sweets, we're gonna get this guy."

"I'm wondering," she said, rubbing her arms. "One of these times, he's going to get lucky."

"They're bringing in our friends in the FBI. We talked about it after you came inside. They're going to go over the security cam footage from the airport. They managed to get ahold of Agent Moreno while we were standing there. Glad to know we're safe."

"What good will that do?"

"This is a Federal issue. They can bring in high-powered explosive experts for one thing."

It broke David's heart to see her so hopeless. He moved next to her and took her into his arms. "They might be able to see the guy slip the stuff in your bag. They have facial recognition software. If he's ever been arrested, they'll have him on file. They'll put out a BOLO. They'll get him."

"That's a lot of ifs." She rubbed her hands together. "May I use your phone? I'm going to call Janice."

David was glad Paula wasn't usually prone to weeping, for if a situation ever called for it, this was it. He was also glad, considering the number of times he'd given in to the impulse to hold Paula in his arms, that he wasn't engaged to Sherrie any longer.

The police and the press were on their side. For now. Hopefully, they would have a few days of peace.

Paula was able to get in touch with Janice, and they set a breakfast meeting for the next morning. Luckily, she knew Joe's Café. Apparently, it was a famous landmark.

His partner then showered while he ate his pizza. Afterward, they settled down to form a plan of attack.

"We're meeting Janice at eight. Fortunately, she doesn't live too far away. She's in Costa Mesa, wherever that is," she said.

"If she doesn't give us any other leads to follow up, I think we need to meet with Moreno and Forrest to see about getting the case documents from when your dad brought down the drug operation," said David.

"Aren't they going to be at the airport?"

"I think they'll have some other people handling that. They told me they want to meet with us tomorrow. Maybe they can expedite your getting a new ID, too. I'll take care of getting a new car while you meet with Janice."

"No. I want you there. You might think of something to ask her that I won't. And she can probably drive us to a car rental place and save you lots of bother."

"All right. As long as you don't think I'll be intruding." He stroked her cheek with his knuckles, not liking the tragic look in her eyes.

* * *

David and Paula noticed a heavy marine haze had settled on Laguna Beach the next morning as they walked to Joe's Café. They held hands, and David was glad to see that Paula seemed to have been refreshed by her sleep. Unfortunately, he hadn't been. He kept thinking about the man who had condemned them to death. He had to appear confident in front of Paula, but this last incident had been the closest call yet.

Janice turned out to be a hefty blonde of about six feet tall. She could be a Federal Marshal herself.

To Paula's evident surprise, the woman greeted her with a hug. "Blythe! You've grown up to be a beauty!" she said. "I'm so sorry you're having this trouble."

"You're so good to come and meet me. This is my friend, David," said Paula.

They shook hands.

Paula's brow gathered. "I'm so sorry about your father. I feel like it's all my fault. He was just trying to protect me."

"That was his job, you know," said Janice, wiping a tear from the corner of her eye. "He was a really good man."

Paula introduced David and said, "I'm a TV journalist now, as your dad probably told you. I'm David's partner. We're hoping to get the whole gang this time and expose their guilt to the public."

A waitress led them to a booth and handed them menus. David was pleased to see it was a man's sort of breakfast place. "I'll have the Monterey omelet with a side of biscuits and gravy," he said to the waitress who looked to be in her seventies.

"I'll just have an English muffin," said Paula, handing the menu back to their server.

"I'd like the French toast," said Janice with a smile. "Thank you."

When the waitress had gone, Paula said, "Tell me everything you can remember about me."

"Well, you were pretty quiet," Janice said. "Looking back, I realize you must have been severely traumatized."

"Did I ever talk about what happened?"

"No. But you might have to your therapist. You liked her a lot. When I asked you what a therapist was, I remember you said, "A nice lady who helps me.""

"I don't suppose you remember her name."

David was agreeably surprised when Janice answered. "I do because it was so funny! Dr. Kitchen!"

He asked, "Do you have any idea how old she was back then? Maybe she's still practicing."

"Blythe thought she was pretty, so maybe she was young. I don't know."

David pulled out his phone and started a search. "Do you have any idea where Paula ... Blythe lived?"

"Yeah. She lived right here in an apartment. It was her safe house during the trial, I imagine."

"So the woman probably practiced in Orange County," he said, typing in *Child psychologist Dr. Kitchen Orange County*.

The phone worked for a few minutes before displaying *Dr. Susan Kitchen, Child Psychologist, Orange County, California*. It showed an address and telephone number in Costa Mesa.

"Eureka!" he said. "Apparently, she practices near your home, Janice. Costa Mesa."

Paula held out her hand for the phone and pressed the screen for the call. The office answered.

"Hello, this is Blythe Kensington," Paula said, flashing a look at him. "I am a former patient of Dr. Kitchen's. I would like to schedule a follow-up appointment as soon as possible. I'm here from out of town. My business is urgent."

"May I ask what it concerns?" David could hear the receptionist's voice.

"Dr. Kitchen helped me through a huge trauma when I was a child. I am certain she will remember it. It was front-page news. Just tell her the trauma has resurfaced."

The receptionist asked for her number. David gave it to Paula, who repeated it into the phone.

"I'll call you back as soon as I've spoken with her." The woman terminated the call.

David watched and listened as the two women exchanged remembrances of playing Barbies on the beach. Janice also shared memories of her dad.

His phone rang. Noting the number, he handed it to Paula.

"Blythe Kensington," she answered.

"Can you come this afternoon at one o'clock?" David heard the receptionist say. "Dr. Kitchens has an opening that just came up, and she is most anxious to see you."

"That would be great. Is the address on the internet still correct?"

"Yes. Harbor Boulevard."

"Tell her thanks for making time for me. I'll see you then."

When she had finished, David said, "I forgot to tell you. That's when we're supposed to meet with Agents Moreno and Forrest."

"It's okay. You can meet with them by yourself. I have a feeling this is more important for me to do."

"You're probably right. Janice, do you know of a car rental agency around here?" he asked.

"There's one in Costa Mesa. I can drop you there on my way home. And I won't let you take a cab this afternoon, Blythe. Not when you're going to be in my neighborhood! If it's okay with you, we can visit at my house and then I'll drop you at Dr. Kitchen's."

"Thank you," said Paula. "That would be great."

"Now, why the FBI?" she asked. "Are you in danger from my father's killer?"

Paula and David took turns telling her their story, ending with the explosion the day before.

"But I heard that on the news! They said there were two victims who hadn't been identified yet!"

"A calculated misdirection," said Paula. "The press can be helpful sometimes."

The woman shook her head. "You have been through so much. I'm putting you both on the prayer chain at my church. You need it!"

"We appreciate that," said David.

They had finished their meal, and after another cup of coffee, they payed their tab and Janice led them out to her car. "I assume you need a ride to the car rental?"

* * *

This time they rented another Focus. David dropped Paula off at Janice's apartment and went to meet with Moreno and Forrest at their office at the Federal Building in Santa Ana.

They exchanged greetings. David thought both agents looked tired. Almost as tired as he felt himself.

"Glad to see you're still alive," said Moreno. "How did you end up in Southern California?"

"Paula's idea. She wants to go over the lawyer's files concerning the case her father testified in, and also she wanted to establish contact with someone who knew the Federal Marshal who was killed."

He was wary of telling them anything about the Mason Clinic, Janice, or Dr. Kitchen.

"Do you have someone going over the security tapes at the airport?" he asked.

"Yeah," said Forrest. "Could take a while. You didn't go to baggage claim? You went straight from the Delta flight to the Alamo car rental?"

"Right. It was crazy crowded, though."

"If at all possible, we'll find him," said Moreno. "Now, the other matter. The case files. We can subpoena them. I don't think there will be any problems getting a judge to do that with all the difficulties you've been having. Obviously, the case isn't closed. The court documents are filed with the court, of course. Those may take a little longer to dig out. Like Ms. Kensington's WITSEC case file, they'll be stored off-site."

"How soon can we get the case files?" David asked.

"The Federal Courthouse is right here in Santa Ana," said Moreno. "There is a time from 4:00 on where we can approach the bench and request a subpoena. We'll do that this afternoon. Then we'll go to the U.S. Attorney's Office and present it. They'll probably have the documents by tomorrow afternoon. We'll give you a call."

"What happened at the Mason Clinic?" asked Forrest. "I thought you were due to be there for a couple of weeks, at least."

"Wasn't necessary," said David. "You'll have to talk to Paula about that. I'm not comfortable sharing her information."

"You can't expect us to do our job without all the facts," said Forrest, irritation clear in the tenor of his voice. "Did she remember anything or not?"

"As I said, you'll have to talk to her," David reiterated.

"When can we do that?" the agent asked. "I thought she'd be with you today."

"If you get those case documents, she'll want to see them. How about tomorrow afternoon?"

Forrest agreed with bad grace.

"Now," said David. "How about you tell me how anyone could have known we were flying from Minneapolis yesterday? How did they find us so quickly?"

"Porter is still in the wind," said Moreno. "He must have followed you to the airport."

"But how in the world did he even know we were in Minnesota? There's a leak somewhere, and it could very well be in this office. You two knew we were going to the Mason Clinic because you heard my phone conversation with my father. Outside of you, no one knew of our plans except him."

"Good point," said Moreno, turning to gaze at his partner who looked ready to explode. "We made a report when we returned to California. To our Special Agent in Charge. It included that information. Who she told, I don't know."

"May I speak to your SAC?" David asked.

"Sure," said Moreno. He punched his intercom. "Ask Special Agent Raleigh if she is available to meet with David van Pelt about the Kensington/Sutherland case."

A few moments later, the SAC appeared in the office. She was a very attractive woman with prematurely white hair and a trim figure.

"Mr. van Pelt?" she extended her hand. "Special Agent in Charge Carolyn Raleigh."

"Good to meet you," said David. "I'm sorry to tell you, but it seems you have a leak somewhere in this office."

Her features hardened. "Is that so? Explain?" She remained standing, so David stayed on his feet as well.

He repeated what he had told Moreno and Forrest.

"And you told no one but your father?"

"No."

"Well. Someone must have followed you there."

David said with impatience, "That is hardly likely. Billy Porter, the hired assassin, is known us, to the police, and the FBI. He wouldn't risk following us through rural Illinois. We would have spotted him for certain. No. He knew where we were going. He tracked us from the Mason clinic."

"That would mean one of our agents is dirty, and I find that difficult to believe."

"How many agents are in this office, and how many knew the situation?" asked David.

"Moreno and Forrest reported at a weekly meeting when they returned from Indiana."

The two men looked uncomfortable. They had failed to divulge that fact. "We had a BOLO out for Billy Porter. Local agents in Indianapolis were following up on that. They were briefed, of course."

David decided to let her figure out how many ways the information could have leaked. "I'll be waiting to hear from you tomorrow afternoon about the case files," he said to Moreno. Thank you for your time, Special Agent Raleigh."

He exited the Federal Building, steaming. No way was he going to give the FBI any more information. It was as leaky as a sieve.

CHAPTER TWENTY-TWO

Paula was anxious to meet Dr. Kitchen and was very glad she had such an early appointment. Her office on Harbor Boulevard was tucked into a corner of a large medical building with windows onto a greenbelt in back. She was interested to see if she remembered the doctor.

Paula was greeted by the cheerful receptionist whom she had spoken with on the phone. She only had to wait in the cozy, wood-paneled waiting room for a few minutes before Dr. Kitchen opened her door and invited her back to her office. The room had two overstuffed green corduroy couches facing one another. Paula seated herself on the one facing the picture window of the greenbelt. There were orchids on a coffee table between the couches.

The doctor herself was dressed in a black pantsuit with an ivory blouse, her shiny black hair drawn up on top of her head in a haphazard bun.

Smiling at Paula, she said, "I see you have grown up to be a remarkably beautiful woman, Blythe. You are the image of your mother with those lovely cheekbones."

"Thank you. I wish I could remember you as well as you remember me," Paula said. "My WITSEC name is Paula James. Do you think you could call me that? I think I would be a little more comfortable."

"Certainly. Suppose you tell me what has been going on in your life?"

"WITSEC moved us to rural Missouri. I have very few memories before that time. I went through elementary, middle school and high school there. I received my undergraduate and graduate degrees from Northwestern." She paused, trying to remember that life that now seemed so placid and long ago. "My father farmed, my mother took up watercolors. Now I know that Dad wanted to live on a farm in a small town after all those dangerous years of living undercover in Southern California. But I never knew that until recently. I guess I supposed he had always been a farmer."

She told Dr. Kitchen about her father's undercover work as a meth cook and how she and David had exposed the organization and taken it down.

"Like father like daughter. He must have been very proud of you."

"He was murdered before it happened, unfortunately, and my mom died of bone cancer. There was no one left to tell me about my past. And it has suddenly become very important that I know about it. Someone is trying to murder me."

Paula related her recent history, starting with the murder of the Marshal.

"My goodness, Paula. What a hair-raising time you have had. I can see why you have sought me out. I hope I can help you a bit. You had started to close off the memories of your captivity even when you came to see me."

"Anything you could tell me would be a help."

Dr. Kitchen got up and went to her oaken desk, bringing back a manila folder. "I printed out all my case notes. You are welcome to take them and look through them at your leisure, but I can tell you a few impressions that I remember."

"That would be great," Paula said, reaching for the file.

"When you came to me you were like a little nut in a shell. You sat curled up on the couch, holding your knees to your chest in spite of your casts. You spoke in a tiny voice."

"Sounds like I was a mess."

"You were doing your best to find some safety in the world. I only saw you for a few weeks, while your dad was going through the trial. Your whole arm and your leg beneath your knee were in casts, and you were in pain."

"What did I talk about?"

"You talked a lot about some friend of your mother's. It was a total non sequitur. I think you were concentrating on random facts that had nothing to do with your kidnapping. You went on about how he used to visit the house when your father was undercover."

"He?"

"Yes, he. I must say, I formed the opinion that he was your mother's lover and that you missed him once your father was back."

Paula took in this fact with difficulty. *My mother had a lover while my father was risking his life undercover? I don't believe it.* "What sorts of things did I say about him?"

"He used to take you and your mother to the beach and out for meals. I remember your telling me that he took you to the Ferris wheel on the Santa Monica pier."

"That is one memory that I sort of have," Paula said, grasping at it as she remembered her impression last month when she and David had ridden that Ferris wheel when their former story had brought them to LA. It was the first clue she had that she had ever been in Southern California. But she had supposed one of her parents had taken her.

"You talked about funnel cakes, too. You loved them." The doctor smiled. "They are a favorite of mine, too."

"How long was my father undercover?"

"I learned from your mother that he was gone for two years. That is a long time for a young girl."

"Obviously, I was looking for a father figure," Paula mused.

"Yes. You were seeking happy memories when you talked to me. You even sang some songs your mother used to comfort you. You were very angry with your father for what you saw as deserting you and your mother."

"What about the kidnapping? Do you know if they ever figured out how it happened?" Paula leaned forward on the couch.

"No, they didn't. You were apparently asleep when they took you, but no one knew how they got into the house. You had a pretty sophisticated alarm system. Your parents just woke one morning, and you were gone."

"When we lived in Missouri, I was always terrified that my parents were going to abandon me. I remember that." To Paula's surprise, tears rose in her eyes.

"How do you feel now that they are dead?"

The tears fell. "Abandoned. I know it's unreasonable. Especially since I left home for college years ago."

"But perfectly understandable." The doctor's face and voice were both gentle. "I would only caution you to be careful in your relationships. You don't want to try to replace your parents."

David's face flashed through her mind. Hadn't she worried that she was becoming too dependent on David? Were her feelings for him a result of her recent losses? She cringed, remembering her clinginess.

"I see I have struck a nerve," said her doctor.

"My partner at the TV station where I work. I'm pretty attached to him."

"I would only caution you to take it slowly."

Paula took a deep breath. "Thanks for the advice."

"You can't come out of trauma like the one you went through without some baggage."

Paula found herself telling Dr. Kitchen about her visit to the Mason Clinic and Dr. Adams' decision to leave the past where it was.

"I think she was wise. I only know what your parents told me about what you went through. They only knew from the evidence. I'm sure you have heard it. But I don't think it would be at all healthy or serve any purpose for you to experience it again. Concentrate on building happy, healthy memories."

"Is there anything else you can tell me that would be useful in tracking down whoever is trying to kill me?"

"Everything we discussed is there in the case notes I gave you. Except for telling me about those few happy memories you had before your kidnapping, you didn't really say much. You were quite hostile towards your poor father. I hope you overcame that in time?"

"Yes. But I never loved him as much as I loved my mother. I remember feeling guilty about it because I didn't understand it. He was never anything but good to me."

Dr. Kitchens smiled a gentle smile. "I hope I have helped shed light on that a little bit."

"You have. Thank you very much for seeing me." Paula checked her watch and was dismayed to see she had been talking to the doctor for over an hour. "I'm afraid my purse was burned in the explosion yesterday. I don't have the money to pay you today. Do you take credit cards?"

"I'm not charging you for this hour. It was a privilege I don't often get, being a child psychologist. Best of luck to you, Paula. And if there are any further questions you have, you can reach me by phone. I hope you will be safe. I will be watching the news."

"That's what my therapist at the Mason Clinic said. I hope I don't disappoint you."

"You won't. You're going to come out on top."

* * *

Janice was waiting for her when she got out to the parking lot. "How did it go?" she asked.

"As well as could be expected. I didn't tell her anything about the kidnapping. I had already blocked it out.

"That's too bad. What a disappointment. Are you ready to go meet David?"

"Yes," she said, embarrassment coloring her cheeks. What must David think of her? "Did he call?"

"Yeah. He's all done with the FBI. I suggested we meet at Ruby's at the end of Balboa Beach Pier."

"What's Ruby's?"

"A 50's type hamburger joint. Great fun."

* * *

When Paula saw David, standing outside the restaurant, he was leaning against the rail, looking out to the ocean. The marine haze had evaporated and it was a splendid day. She wanted nothing more than to join him at the railing and put her hand over his.

She resisted the temptation, calling out to him above the cries of the seagulls and the crash of the waves.

Turning around, he smiled at Paula and Janice.

"This is heaven out here. What a great place!" he said.

He followed them inside and Paula excused herself to use the restroom. When she came out, she placed herself next to Janice. David seemed not to notice.

"So how were our friends at the FBI?" she asked.

"Pretty upset with me for telling them they had a leak. I suspect Internal Affairs will get involved. But they're getting a subpoena this afternoon for the case files from the U.S. Attorney and putting in a request for the court files at the Federal Courthouse. How did your meeting with Dr. Kitchen go?"

Paula made a face. "Nothing new, except she thought my mother had a lover while my dad was undercover. Just what I needed to know, right? I don't think I believe her, but I'll never know, will I? She said I'd already shut down by the time I started seeing her."

"That's a bummer," said David.

"Yeah," agreed Janice.

"Remember my feeling about the Ferris wheel on Santa Monica pier? That man was the one who took me there. Dr. Kitchen said he was my father figure."

A waitress came to take their order. Paula ordered fish and chips, while David and Janice chose a burger platter and milkshakes. Realizing she had never even asked Janice about her family, Paula remedied this and learned that her mother was still living and she had a brother in Seattle who worked for Amazon.

Paula kept her talking about herself all during lunch and listened to reminisces of her father, the marshal, who had been a major figure in Janice's life. She was adrift now, having quit her job as an admin for a tech firm in Orange County. She was looking for a new job that would pay the rent while she concentrated on her writing. Paula was intrigued to realize her new friend wrote historical romances.

Janice asked David about his family, and Paula listened as he told about his father who was the rock in his life, his mother having left the family when Dr. van Pelt was doing his residency. For the first time, Paula gave this some thought. Had David's mother deserted them for another man? How had this skewed David's view of marriage?

When they left Ruby's and walked down the pier, David attempted to hold her hand. She folded her arms across her chest. He raised his brows at her. She just smiled at him.

She parted from Janice with a hug, and Paula said, "Please keep in touch, Janice. You have been such a big help. Maybe tomorrow night you and I could have dinner someplace really nice. You choose."

"I don't want to be a wet blanket," said David. "But I don't think you should be making plans. Now that the FBI knows we're alive, we might be in danger again. Remember, someone there is bent."

Paula covered her mouth with her fingers. "Oh! Sorry, Janice. I didn't think! Of course, we don't want to put you in danger!"

"I'll keep in touch by phone," said Janice. "When this is all over, I'll take you up on your offer. We can go to the Crab Cooker. I love that place!"

* * *

"Where to now?" asked Paula once they had seen Janice off and climbed into the Focus.

"I'm going to call Agent Moreno and see if they've had any luck finding our bomber on the airport security cams. Then I think we need to get you a new phone. I don't know what to do about your ID. We'll have to have it when we fly home."

"I have a birth certificate here in California in the name of Blythe Kensington, I imagine. I can check online if you lend me your phone. Maybe it's at the Orange County Courthouse."

She felt tension thrumming through them, and knew David was puzzled by her behavior. But how in the world could she explain to him that she was worried she might be clinging to him because she no longer had a family?

He dialed the FBI and asked for Moreno.

"Any luck with the airport cams?" he asked.

Paula could hear the agent's answer. "Yeah. We got him. We're putting the image through facial recognition software. Hopefully, we'll have an ID on him soon."

"Good news!" said David. "Can you call me if you get a hit?"

"Will do."

David handed her the phone. I'll start driving in the direction of Santa Ana. It may take a while. The traffic in this place is murder."

Paula was able to find her Blythe Kensington birth record online listed in Orange County. After obtaining a copy at the courthouse, they went to the DMV to get her a temporary license, using the address at the B & B where they were staying. It felt peculiar to have a new name.

It was after four o'clock by the time they were finished at the DMV. She wished she weren't joined at the hip with David, but that was the nature of the investigation. It was so hard not to reach for his hand when they were walking or confide in him her fears. The pull she felt towards him was nearly irresistible. It reminded her of oceans and tides.

After they had bought her a phone and a new purse and were sitting in a very authentic looking Mexican restaurant, David got a call from Agent Moreno.

He put it on speaker with the volume on low enough not to bother the other early diners.

"We got the subpoena from the judge for the lawyer's records and delivered it. They said they'd have a clerk get right on it and have them for us tomorrow morning."

"Great," said David. "Thanks. Okay if we come to your office at 9:00 tomorrow morning?"

"Yeah. I'll be here. We had some luck on the bomber, too. Name of Oscar Moran. He did time for drug trafficking in the same gang we prosecuted in Ms. James's father's case. Looks like he's graduated into a paid assassin. We've got a BOLO out on him. Where are you now?"

"Having dinner in Santa Ana at Benito's. Couple blocks from you."

"We'll put a guy on you, just in case Moran gets tabs on you again."

"Wonderful," said David. "Bye for now." Once he had hung up, he said, "Just another day in the life of an investigative journalist."

"It's getting tiring, I admit," said Paula. "I wonder if I should be going by my real name, now that I've gotten ID as Blythe."

"Do you feel like a Paula or a Blythe?"

"I don't know. I think I need to shake up things in my life. Nothing ever happens to me," she scooped a nacho.

"You're going to be ready for a cruise to the Caribbean when this is over."

"You know that sounds dull, right?"

"Don't you ever relax?"

"No more than you do. I think you inherited your dad's work ethic."

"Okay. . . Why did *you* decide to be an investigative journalist?" David asked, finishing off his *burrito grande*.

"For the glamorous travel," she said. "I might never have seen Santa Ana otherwise."

"No. I'm serious," he said.

"My life was dull in Missouri. While I was at Northwestern, I just got the j-bug. Then, like everyone else in j-school, I read *All the President's Men*."

"You're a regular Woodward. I'm Bernstein. Seriously, you have a knack for it. Another great read is *The Pelican Brief*."

"I think we can write our own thrillers," she said. "Now, if only I looked like Julia Roberts."

"You've got to know you're hot, Paula," he said, his eyes dancing.

She blushed fiercely. "You shouldn't say things like that."

"Why not? It's the truth."

"You don't want me getting the wrong idea," she said lightly. "Now, unless I am misreading him, I think our new good-guy tail has arrived. "Let's make tracks. It's been a long day, and I want to get in a walk on the beach before I completely lose my energy."

* * *

Paula changed out of her investigative clothes into leggings and a hoodie. As she came out of the bathroom, she said, "I'm going for a walk."

"Wait a minute for me to change, and I'll join you."

Since the purpose of the walk was for her to get away from David for long enough to think about the realities of their relationship, she said, "I need to be alone for a while if you don't mind."

His brows came together. "What's wrong?"

"Nothing. Dr. Kitchen just gave me some things to think about and I haven't had a chance to process them."

"Does that have anything to do with why you're treating me like a leper?"

"Please, David. Don't go there. I'll see you in a bit."

Paula walked across the street and down the stairs to the beach. Despite her stated desire for a walk, she immediately sat down in the sand. As she ran her fingers through the soft grains, she realized that this could very well be the beach that she had come to with Janice and her father.

What was it about beaches that was such a draw? With the evening fog hugging the rocky shore and the small cove where she sat, she felt like she finally had the proportions right. Sea=huge. Paula=tiny.

Perhaps she shouldn't take herself so seriously. Perhaps it didn't matter why she was attracted so strongly to David. On the other hand, she cringed when she thought about how her first thought when her father was murdered was to go to David. And when she was in his presence, she knew everything was going to be all right. As she always told herself: David calms the crazies.

He wasn't anything father-like. He was irreverent and funny. Her father had been withdrawn and serious.

What had the man been like who Dr. Kitchen had told her about? She vaguely recalled being excited when they went on the Ferris wheel. She couldn't imagine her father ever taking her on the Ferris wheel.

The unknown man must have made a real impression if she had talked about him to her therapist rather than talking about the kidnapping. If she had been dissociating from that experience, she would have chosen happy memories. Thus, she could safely assume she associated the man in her mind with happiness.

As I do David.

But surely it wasn't wrong to want happiness? But wasn't she also relying on David for safety from unhappiness? No one could give you that.

She was floundering here. Maybe what Dr. Kitchen had been telling her was not to rely on someone else for your happiness. Not to grab for it. Not to expect someone else to give you the unconditional love that a father might offer.

At that moment, she saw movement from the rocks that rose from the ocean to her right. Against the bright western sky, there was a dark shape facing her. Someone in a wetsuit? Without conscious thought, she threw herself flat on the sand, just as a shot flew over her head.

Paula screamed.

She heard another shot. This one was coming from the top of the steps. Her guard!

Booted feet clattered down the steps.

"Are you all right Ms. James?"

"Is he gone?"

"He dove into the sea. Let's get you inside now. It's dangerous out here in the open."

She ran up the stairs two at a time and straight into David's waiting arms.

"What's going on?" he demanded. "I heard a shot."

"Someone was shooting at me from the rocks."

With an arm around her, he shepherded her across the street and into their B & B.

"That was really stupid, Paula," he said. "You made yourself a target."

"I know it was dumb, okay?" She shrugged off his arm, though what she really wanted to do was to cuddle next to him.

"What is the matter with you?" he asked, his voice angry.

She wished there was a room to disappear into. Paula plopped down on one of the couches. "I'm just strung out, okay? Someone is trying to kill us, and I'm trying to figure out my past. It's a little overwhelming."

David slammed out of the studio to speak to their guard.

She took the file she had received from Dr. Kitchen and went into the bathroom. Sitting in the dry tub, she began shaking in the aftermath of yet another attempt to kill her. *David would be holding me if I hadn't been such a brat.*

For half an hour she sat and shook and tried to process what she knew and what she needed to know. For the first time, she realized it might be an impossible task to find who wanted her dead before he succeeded with his task.

No! I can't start thinking like that!

She had to find the main bad guy and get this whole ordeal over with! Maybe Dr. Kitchen's notes would help her. She forced herself to open the file and began to read.

Blythe is a clearly traumatized girl of nine years old who has been kidnapped, physically abused, and shows signs of starvation. When I ask about her ordeal, she stares at me blankly and then starts singing Negro spirituals or talking about her mother and a man who may have been her lover. I have deduced that he was around a lot when her father was undercover.

She typifies the abandoned child—exceedingly withdrawn, fantasizes about her relationships with parents and how much they love her, lives in her own little world. Add to that all the trauma she has been through, and I don't know what will become of her through the years. I have seldom seen such a difficult case. She is destined to have a victim mentality with good reason.

Paula's heart broke for the child she had been. Nevertheless, she had grown up strong, hadn't she? Her parents deserved a lot of credit for raising her to be self-sufficient and to have an idea of her own worth. To her, it was a blessing that she didn't remember that time of great trauma and she was very glad Dr. Adams had discerned that and hadn't proceeded with the attempt to resurrect those memories.

The further reports were more of the same. However they did include the name "Uncle Renny" as the family friend. Whatever had happened to the man? Had he stopped visiting once her father had returned?

Putting the five reports back into the file, she climbed out of the tub and opened the door to go back into the studio.

"I'm sorry, Paula," David said. "I was a jerk. I was just so scared."

"It's all right," she said. "I need to stand on my own two feet anyway."

She thrust the file at him. "You should probably read this. Then it won't surprise you what a hot mess I am."

"Whoever said you were a hot mess?" David asked, his voice like a growl. "I don't think so at all. You're brave and determined."

"Just read the stupid file," she said. "I'm going to bed."

Retreating to the bathroom again, she washed her face, brushed her teeth, and changed into her new pair of Wonder Woman PJs.

When she came out, David looked up from his reading. "This is a bunch of garbage," he said. "She was looking for what she thought she should see. So what if you wanted to keep things to yourself? Why should you tell someone who was a complete stranger?"

Paula felt something shift in her chest and click into place. "You could be right. I didn't think of it that way." She stood taller. "That file makes me feel as weak as a Twinkie."

"She was wrong to show it to you. You may have been nine years old, but you had your own personality, your own way of doing things. And you've grown up to be capable and smart and brave. The furthest thing from a victim I can imagine."

"You don't think I'm . . . that I'm needy?" she asked in a small voice.

His brow lowered. "Paula, come here," he said in a no-nonsense tone. "Is that what you think? That you're somehow supposed to be superhuman? That you're not entitled to be scared someone is trying to kill you?"

She ignored his entreaty, so he came to her instead and folded her into his arms next to his heart. "We're human, sweets. We all need each other. It's the way the world works. That 'no man is an island' bit."

"You're so romantic," she said with a little chuckle.

"I am, actually." Putting a finger under her chin, he lifted it and bent down to kiss her. It wasn't a brotherly kiss or a fatherly kiss. He kissed her like he couldn't get enough of her; like he was suddenly a starving man.

Paula felt desired and cared about. David was home in a way she had never experienced it. The feeling pushed out all the self-doubts she had been nurturing. "You calm the crazies," she said. "You always have."

"You do the same for me, Paula-Blythe. But I have my own worries about this relationship. Am I enough for you? Am I a louse because I'm not heartbroken over Sherrie?"

"Is that what you think?" she asked, stunned.

"You don't think I'm on the rebound?"

"It never occurred to me. I didn't really know how seriously to take you."

"I think you *should* take me seriously."

"I have a little secret to tell you," she said, playing with the placket of his shirt.

"And it is ...?"

"I've been pretty mushy about you since I was an undergrad. Five years. This isn't a sudden thing for me."

"Really? You're kidding me! And here I thought you had a thing for Aubrey."

"We dated, but it was a one-way street. I didn't return his feelings. It was always you."

"Hot dog!" he said, giving her a high five.

"But we're not going to do anything about this now. Like sleep together or anything," said Paula. "Feelings are running too high. Neither of us should commit to anything while this is going on. It would be foolish."

He grimaced. "I suppose you're right. But I want you to know you're my main squeeze. And I never felt this way about Sherrie. All this is completely new to me."

In spite of all they faced, Paula felt contentment curl through her. "I haven't even asked you how your chest is feeling," she said, putting her head over his bandage.

"Almost good as new. But, I'm glad we have someone watching out for us. You scared me to death, sitting there like a target on the beach."

"I won't do it again, okay? Now, let's drop it and watch the news or something."

He waggled his eyebrows. "I vote for 'something.'"

She punched his arm. "The news it is." She walked over and grabbed the remote. They cuddled together on the couch, and she flicked on the TV.

The news features concerned local politics, environmental disasters, and a tiny segment of national news. During the commercial break, there was a political ad for the upcoming primary election. A good-looking man with great hair and deep blue eyes spoke about his vast experience in politics and his suitability to fill the office of a U.S. Senator.

Paula sat stunned. His name was Renwood Fullmer.

"It's him, David. 'Uncle Rennie.' The man who took me on the Ferris wheel. The one Dr. Kitchen thought was having an affair with my mother. Talk about a silver tongue. As the British would say, 'butter wouldn't melt in his mouth.'"

"I don't like him," David said. "He's too slick. He's not a person; he's a production."

"But can't you see how he would captivate a nine-year-old girl with that smile of his?"

"I suppose. He probably wasn't such a political animal back then."

"I have to get in touch with him! I wonder if the police or our lawyers questioned him? He might know something!"

"Well, we'll find out tomorrow. We're getting the case notes, remember?"

CHAPTER TWENTY-THREE

David couldn't sleep. It didn't help that Paula was right there, in the next bed. Imagine that! She'd had a crush on him for five years. What an ignoramus he was. How could he have missed it?

Once again, he had the desire to take her away to Iceland or somewhere equally remote. The thought of how close that bullet came to hitting her scared him through. Kirk, their guard, said she threw herself into the sand at the last possible second.

Who was dirty in the FBI? Was it Moreno with his long connection to the case? Or was it the irritable Forrest who asked more questions than he gave answers? Or could it be their SAC or one of the other agents in the office?

Someone had an agent under his thumb. What had Marshal Sutherland known that had caused him to be killed? For that matter, what did Paula know? The questions wouldn't let him be. He had to find the answers before someone killed the love of his life.

* * *

They had the U.S. Attorney's files in response to the subpoena by ten o'clock the next morning. Moreno offered a couple of desks at the FBI headquarters for them to go through the files.

Moreno himself was the subject of one of the first interviews, as he was on the team that rescued Paula. He described the series of events leading to the rescue. David offered to read this account himself so that it wouldn't add to Paula's distress.

The FBI had run the property ownership records of every single offender that Paula's father, Chet Kensington, had dealings with while he was undercover. They had visited the properties, one by one. Since Chet knew which names were real and which names were aliases he had been vital to this part of the operation. When this search didn't turn up anything, they had run searches on the aliases. They had finally found Blythe when they ran searches on relatives of the known offenders. She had been located at a cabin in the San Gabriel mountains belonging to the ex-wife of one of the men in custody. She had been arrested and charged as an accessory to kidnapping. As part of a plea deal, she had revealed a number of other offenders that she had met during the years she was married.

David was struck by what a valuable operative Paula's father had been. There were pages and pages of data related to the search. During his undercover years, the man had reaped volumes of information.

The men who were found in the cabin where Paula was were being held were on death row in Terre Haute Federal Prison in Indiana. They would have no reason to hire a hit man, as they had already been convicted.

David noted the name of the staff attorney who had done the questioning. He sent a text to Moreno. *Is Frederick Almora still practicing? Could Paula and I arrange an interview with him?*

He received a return text a moment later. *Almora is retired, but he's a great guy. This case was a highlight of his career. I bet he'd talk to you. Especially if you offer to buy him dinner.*

David thanked Moreno and then spoke to Paula who was wading her way through interrogatories. "You know, the best way to get the highlights of this case would be to talk to the U.S. Staff Attorney who did all the work." He told Paula about Moreno's text.

"That sounds like a good idea. I don't even know what I'm looking for here."

David was already texting Moreno for Almora's contact information.

* * *

When David and Paula met Frederick Almora in The Five Crowns steakhouse that evening, they weren't exactly sure what to expect. Their guest turned out to be short and round with a frizz of white hair like a crown around his head. With sharp, birdlike eyes, he surveyed the two of them as though sizing them up.

"So you're Blythe Kensington, all grown up!" he said, extending his hand to her. It was surprisingly large and firm.

"Yes, I am," she said with a smile. "Though for now, I'm still using my WITSEC name of Paula James. Thank you so much for meeting us tonight. This is my TV partner David van, Pelt. We work for WOOT TV in Chicago."

David offered his hand, and the attorney shook it.

A hostess in a black cocktail dress appeared. "Is your party ready to be seated now?" she asked.

"We are," David told her.

The hostess led them to a cozy alcove that reminded David of a high-end English pub.

"I love this place," said Almora. "It's got class and great prime rib."

David was glad Moreno had given him a good dining tip.

A waiter appeared to take their cocktail orders. David was still taking antibiotics and felt he should be cautious, so he ordered tonic and lime. Paula ordered white wine, and their guest ordered Scotch.

"I'm very disturbed to hear of the threats on your life, Ms. James. Although, I must say I'm not surprised."

"It's Paula, please Mr. Almora. Can you tell us why you're not surprised?"

"I'm Fred," he said. "I always figured there was more to that organization than the ones we caught. Someone thinks you saw something, and for them to react so extremely makes it obvious there's a lot at stake for this person."

"Please share your thoughts. We've been going through the U.S. Attorney files, and we are finding it pretty slow-going," said Paula. "We thought maybe you could give us an overview."

"Have you ever heard the expression 'silver and lead?'"

David said, "Money and bullets. The carrot and the stick. How the drug lords manage their underlings."

"Right. With your dad's testimony, we were able to round up all the little guys and the next two tiers of bosses from Mexico to Seattle. But when the big bosses refused to plea bargain in exchange for the identity of the big boss, they claimed there wasn't one."

"Couldn't they have been telling the truth?" asked Paula.

"Not on your life. They were all scared spitless. They wouldn't have been if they didn't fear the lead."

The waiter reappeared for their orders. All of them ordered the prime rib, Yorkshire pudding, green beans, and horseradish. David was glad Paula was finally getting a decent meal. She was getting so thin the skin on her face was almost as transparent as onion skin.

"Whoever was managing them, still is. Except for the kidnappers, they're all in supermax security prison in Florence, Colorado. Yet one of them ended up dead just last year. Under the strictest confidence, he was trying for a plea deal. He hinted at the identity of the Big Man."

"But word got out?" asked Paula.

Fred nodded.

"Does anyone have any idea how?" David asked, sipping his tonic.

"Must have been a bent guard or someone on the outside who was in on the negotiations."

"So this guy, whoever he is, really has power up in the higher echelons of law enforcement," mused Paula. "A lawyer maybe? Or a judge?"

"Could be," said Fred. "It wouldn't surprise me. Some of the upper-level guys we put away were real leaders in the community. The silver must have been real tempting. But it takes a lot of money to live in Orange County these days. Seattle, San Francisco, too."

"Yeah," said David. "I understand Real Estate is insane."

"Not just that. Some of the men we put away said they had kids they were putting through Stanford, Yale, Harvard . . . Some of them had wives or kids who were sick with huge medical bills."

"There's something wrong in a society when things like that drive people to crime," said Paula, and David was glad that she knew her father had actually been undercover when he'd turned to crime the last year before his death.

Fred said, "Everyone's entitled. No one thinks they should have to deny themselves anything in this part of the world."

The waiter brought their food, and for a few minutes they gave themselves up to the succulent tenderness of the prime rib with horseradish sauce.

David suddenly wished all of this were over and that he and Paula could have a normal relationship where they could travel, sightsee, and eat great meals like this without the threat of violence hanging over them. He longed to be able to trust people again, to look upon law enforcement as the good guys, not possible turncoats.

He knew that their appointed FBI angel was sitting at another table in this restaurant, and hoped he was enjoying a good meal.

"Another thing that points to there being higher brains at work was the jailbreak."

"I haven't come across anything like that in my research, yet," said Paula.

"It was a long time ago. During the trial," Fred said.

"What happened?"

"The men on trial were being held in a federal holding cell in Santa Ana, near the Federal Courthouse. They were some of the top guys, the ones who I think knew the identity of the real drug lord." Fred took a bite of Yorkshire pudding. "It was like something out of a thriller. There was an explosion in the street. Men in ski masks threw open the van doors, killed the guards, and took the prisoners—who were manacled hand and foot—and slung them over their backs. There were three prisoners and about six of the masked guys. They disappeared down a manhole right there in the street."

"Oh my gosh," said Paula. "What happened after that? Were they ever recovered?"

Fred drew out the suspense as he chewed his dinner. "Fortunately, there were SWAT teams in the vehicles before and after the transportation van. We had expected some kind of attempt would be made. They were down that manhole before you could count to ten. They had a shootout. I guess it was real 'old west.'"

"What happened?" David asked. He wondered how often Fred had dined out on this story.

"The good guys were wearing body armor, so they won. One of the prisoners got caught in the crossfire and was killed, but the other two were recovered and sent back to the holding cell."

"It does sound a little Tom Clancy," said Paula.

"Oh, it was lots of fun," said Fred drily. "So, tell me about your adventures. When did you first know someone was gunning for you, Paula?"

"When Marshall Sutherland was murdered on his way to see me in Chicago. You must have known him."

"Yes. I did. He was a good man. That was bad news."

"We thought we were off the grid after that," said David, "but the assassin caught up with us in Indianapolis. There were a couple of attempts there. The perp was caught and then escaped."

"Scene shifts to California. Someone else takes over," said Paula. "He tried to blow us up, and then shot at me on the beach last night. Now we have an FBI minder."

"What no one seems to realize, is that, for the most part, Paula has lost her memory of all the events that took place back then. She's not a danger to anyone."

"The ironic part is that now we have to find this drug lord, whereas before we probably wouldn't have," said Paula.

"Probably is the operative word. You *are* reporters."

"True," David acknowledged. "Once Marshal Sutherland told Paula she was in WITSEC, she wanted to know the story."

"So," said Paula. "Who do you think we're looking for?"

"Someone brilliant, charming, and the last person anyone would suspect," said Fred.

"Are there any clues at all? What about the guy in prison who was ready to flip?" David asked. "Did he give anything away before he was killed?"

"He did say that we only managed to shut down one of his operations. He has one that operates primarily in the Chicago area and another that covers Arizona, Nevada, and Utah, up to Canada."

"That's bad news," said Paula. "No wonder he had a handy thug in Chicago. We know his identity, by the way, but he escaped from jail."

"Anyone do a search of his place?"

"I have no idea," said Paula. "I suppose that's something we should follow up on. He's wanted for the murder of the marshal, as well as arson and attempted murder of David and me."

"You said that 'for the most part' you don't remember what happened. Is there any chance you remember anything about your stay in that cabin when you were held?"

"I had a nightmare about the accident on the way up to the mountains, and some impressions of the cabin, but nothing else."

Fred said, "I have a theory that The Man was using that place as a headquarters for a while. I think you may have seen him coming and going. I'll bet you a buck that's why he thinks you would recognize him on the street."

"Apparently I resemble the way my mother looked at the time of the trial. The marshal saw me on TV. When he learned my parents were dead, he got in touch with me because he thought I would be in danger if The Man saw the broadcast."

"And the marshal was right," said David, suddenly weary. "I don't suppose you'd like to get up close and personal with penguins? I hear it's charming in Tiera del Fuego this time of year."

"Have you considered hypnosis?" asked Fred.

"We have," said David. "Let's just say the outcome was alarming and not helpful."

"Well, I don't think going through the case files or the court files will yield anything I haven't told you. Most of the witnesses took the fifth. Your father's testimony is what convicted every single one of them. He was a very brave man. Forgive me for asking, but how did he die?"

"He went undercover in another drug scenario where we lived in Missouri. He was murdered."

"I'm sorry to hear that," said Fred, and he did seem genuinely sorry.

The waiter appeared to ask about dessert. They all declined, and the server left their check.

"If I were you," said Fred, "I would get the FBI to touch base with the Chicago police. Tell them you have information about a Chicago drug ring and believe this would-be assassin of yours to be connected. See if they have found anything at his residence that might tie him to his boss back here."

"That's a really great suggestion. Thanks," said Paula. "It was good of you to come and meet with us."

"Thanks for dinner."

They all stood and walked to the foyer where they shook hands. "You be in touch if you have any questions," Fred said.

"Well, that sure saved us a lot of hours," said Paula. "I'm going to call Agent Moreno in the morning with that tip he gave us."

"Good. I would suggest a stroll, but I think until we wrap up our business here, we had better forget long periods of time in the open."

"Back to the B & B then," said Paula.

"Did you ever see 'It Happened One Night?'"

"Yes," she said laughing. "Do we need to put up a clothesline between us?"

"It might save me a lot of aggravation."

"I'm sorry, David," she said, linking her arm with his. "I'll wear a gunny sack."

"That wouldn't help. I have a powerful imagination, I'm afraid." He flashed the light on his key ring which was the signal for their FBI angel to approach and look over their car for explosives.

He was a young, eager man with slicked back black hair and a tight smile named Agent Burrows. "Thanks for dinner," he said. "A nice change from McDonald's."

Their car was declared clean by Burrows, and they drove down Pacific Coast Highway toward Laguna and their B & B.

CHAPTER TWENTY-FOUR

Paula could have used a clothesline that night herself. She would very much like to be held, and just imagining David in the other pull-out bed turned her insides to goo. She tried to put all those thoughts in a box, tie it up with a bow, and press on with the case, but it was difficult.

She found her mind straying to the Ferris wheel and her girlhood memory. Was Renwood Fullmer, the Senatorial candidate really the man from her childhood whom she had wanted to be her father? What was he like? Maybe she should look him up and thank him for making a little girl so happy. Was there any chance that he knew something that could help their investigation?

She fell asleep on that thought.

* * *

There was a bright light shining in her eyes. It hurt. She couldn't see anyone around her but the light.

"Hold up that broken arm!" a voice commanded. "Now talk like we told you."

"Mommy and Daddy, please come and get me. My arm hurts so bad. And I'm so hungry, Where are you? These men are mean to me. I don't understand why you won't come!" Tears streamed down her face.

"Excellent," said a familiar voice. She couldn't see who it belonged to.

One of the men who smelled bad came and pulled her off the chair by her bad arm. He threw her in a corner where she cried and cried. Blythe didn't know why this was happening. Didn't her mommy and daddy love her anymore? Had she done something really naughty?

Paula woke up crying bitterly. She felt forlorn and hopeless. Her arm hurt. Her leg hurt. She didn't think anything would ever be right again.

Then there was David sitting on the edge of the bed. "What is it, Paula? What's wrong.

"Nightmare," she croaked.

He gathered her into his arms. "I'm sorry, You were crying like your heart had broken."

"I think maybe it did, back then. I was in the cabin, and I was in pain and hungry. They were hurting me. I couldn't understand why my parents couldn't come and get me. I begged and begged, but they didn't come."

David was holding her tight against his chest. "I don't think that feeling of abandonment has ever left you. It was seared on your soul."

"People leave," she said.

"God doesn't," David said.

"How do you know?" she asked belligerently.

"Sometimes we have to suffer, just like He did, but He knows suffering. Eventually, He relieves it, either by sending someone as He did with you, or by taking you home to Himself."

Paula thought about this. "What you and I have—how can I count on it?"

"I would like to say I'll never leave you, but I've almost died twice in the last month. I want you to trust me, but the one you should cling to is God."

Paula felt as though she were being tossed in the sea by giant waves. One time that had actually happened to her and she had been afraid to go in the ocean again. The ocean was for looking at, not swimming in.

"I think I'd rather not have you in the first place than lose you."

"Too late," he said, stroking her hair. He pulled her onto his lap. "You have me good."

"When did you become religious?" she wanted to know.

"When my mom left. But I have trouble trusting, too. That's probably why I haven't let myself fall for you for the last five years."

This was news.

"Explain," she said.

"I knew when I first met you that you were a forever type of girl. I was afraid you would be my downfall. That you would open me up and then leave like my mom did."

"But what about Sherrie? You opened yourself up to her."

"All Sherrie knew was the celebrity, and that's the way I liked it. I'm just now realizing that. It's good you've wanted to take things slowly. Otherwise, it would have spooked me."

"It seems that we care for one another most unwillingly."

David laughed. "Like Elizabeth and Darcy."

"You've read *Pride and Prejudice?*"

"Saw the mini-series. One of my girlfriends insisted on it."

"You know what I think?" asked Paula. "I think that it's only when you can open yourself to the potential of pain that you can open yourself to love."

"Yes," said David. "Love is an act of faith."

"Maybe I'll have my happy ending when we catch the guy who did all those things to me. Justice will be restored."

"That's why I do the job I do," confessed David. "But everyone won't achieve justice in this life."

"This man will," she said with sudden certainty. "He's going to make a mistake and then we're going to get him."

"Now you're sounding more like yourself," David said.

"It helps to have a partner. I couldn't do this without you."

He kissed her briefly. "I think tomorrow is going to be a busy day. Let's get some sleep. Do you think you can fall asleep if I hold you?"

"Yes. Thank you, David."

* * *

Paula woke in David's arms and wondered at it for a minute. Then she remembered the broken little girl in her dream and realized that he was a gift given to that little girl. Better late than never. She remembered a phrase she had heard, "The mills of God grind slowly, but they grind exceedingly fine."

She kissed David's cheek and then climbed out of the hide-a-bed. It was ten o'clock!

She showered and put on one of the new outfits she had purchased at The Fashion Mall in Indianapolis—turquoise cropped pants, a fitted white shirt piped in turquoise, and a turquoise cardigan. She examined the roots of her blond hair. They were beginning to show light brown. She had dyed it as a disguise, but now she liked it. She would have Chrissy do a weave when this investigation was at an end. In the meantime, it was okay in a messy bun on the top of her head.

When she got out of the bathroom, David was up and on the phone. Seeing her, he put it on speaker. He was explaining to Agent Moreno what they had found out about the other drug organizations in Chicago and the mountain west.

"So this means Billy Porter is probably on the same payroll as the guys were who are now in prison in Colorado. Could you check with the investigation in Chicago concerning him and see if they searched his home? If so could we get an inventory?"

"Good idea," said Moreno. "Will do."

When he hung up, he gave a wolf whistle at Paula's appearance. "You look oh-so-fine."

"Thanks."

"What do you want to do this morning?"

Paula sat down across from where he sat in his sweats. "It's only a whim, and I don't think it would further the investigation, but I'd like to meet Renwood Fullmer, the guy who's running for Senate. I want to find out if he is really the guy who was my father figure when Dad was undercover. He might have stayed close to the family before we went into WITSEC. He may know something that would help us. I know it's a long shot."

"I'll look him up on my phone." A moment later, he said, "Okay. Here he is. He's a senior partner at Howell, Oakley, and Fullmer. This gives his age as fifty-three. Sounds about right. I'll look up his firm."

The listing yielded an office address in Newport Beach and a phone number.

Paula called the number and spoke to the receptionist. "My name is Blythe Kensington, and I would like to speak to Mr. Fullmer about a personal matter. It shouldn't take too long.

"Mr. Fullmer is a very busy man. Could you give me an idea of why you wish to speak to him? I will, of course, keep it confidential."

Paula paused for a moment, then decided to go for broke. "I have lost my memory, but I recognized Mr. Fullmer from a campaign ad on TV. I believe he was a good friend to my family when I was little. I just wanted to find out if he could help me remember anything. I know it is a long shot, but I thought I would give it a try."

"As I said he is a very busy man. His week is fully booked," said the receptionist. "I will give Mr. Fullmer your message, and if he remembers you or your family, he can call you back, and you can make your own arrangements to see him."

"That would be perfect," said Paula. She gave the receptionist her number. "Thank you for your help."

She heard David in the shower when she hung up, so she reassembled the hide-a-beds, and cleaned up around their studio. When her phone rang, she jumped. Could it be Renwood Fullmer already?

"Hello?"

"Is this Blythe?"

"Yes."

"This is Renwood Fullmer. I believe you used to know me as 'Uncle Rennie.' But my receptionist said you had lost your memory."

"Oh, I'm so happy to hear from you. Your receptionist said you were fully booked. Thank you for taking the time to call me back."

"I am anxious to see you. Would you like to have lunch today? I have a break before I have to be in court."

"That would be great! Can I meet you somewhere?"

"How about Shoots? It's a Chinese restaurant near the courthouse in Santa Ana."

"That sounds perfect. I love Chinese," said Paula. "I'd like to bring someone for you to meet if that's okay. He's helping me put together my memory and is sort of my emotional support."

"A boyfriend, eh?" Uncle Rennie chuckled.

"I guess I should start calling him that," she said.

"Sure. I'd love to meet your boyfriend. Will 11:30 be too early for you? That will give us time to talk. I have to be in court at one o'clock."

"Perfect. I'll see you then, Uncle Rennie."

David came in on the tail end of her conversation. The phone was still on speaker. She blushed.

"I've always thought boyfriend was an adolescent term," he said.

"Me, too," said Paula with a laugh. "Too bad you don't have a letterman jacket and a skateboard."

"What I really need is a Corvette."

"Yeah," she said. "You'd look awesome in a Corvette. But I guess we'll have to make do with our little Ford Focus."

* * *

Shoots turned out to be fairly fancy with white tablecloths and sprays of fresh flowers at each table. Men and women dressed for court were talking and laughing, and the atmosphere was jovial.

Paula felt a little strange in her capris. But as soon as she saw Uncle Rennie standing waiting for them, looking handsome with his silver hair and Italian suit, she lost her self-consciousness.

"Hello, Uncle Rennie!" Then she colored. "I suppose you don't want me to call you that anymore."

"Ren will do," he said with a laugh. "Is this your plus one?"

"Yes. I'd like you to meet my partner at WOOT TV, David van Pelt. David, this is Mr. Renwood Fullmer, a very good friend of my family."

The men shook hands, and then Ren gave her a solid hug. "WOOT TV, eh? Has anyone told you how much you resemble your mother?"

"Yes," she said. "But you should know, she just died a couple of months ago. Cancer."

"Oh." Ren's face became suddenly stark as all good cheer vanished from it. "I am so sorry to hear that. Did she suffer?"

"Yes. A lot. For what seemed like a long time."

They followed a Chinese man dressed in black dress pants and a white jacket to a table overlooking a fenced garden with bamboo, an artificial stream, and little ceramic replicas of Chinese temples. The man handed them each a heavy leather encased menu.

"What is the very best thing to eat here?" Paula asked.

"The garlic shrimp is my favorite. Why don't we all get something different? The food comes on big platters we put in the middle, and we can each get a plate and share."

Following this practical suggestion, they each settled on a dish and ordered.

"And your father? He is well, I hope?"

"No, he passed soon after my mother. They were very devoted," she said. She wondered at herself for sugar-coating the truth, but decided murder was not a nice lunchtime topic. Neither was cancer, for that matter.

"Where did WITSEC end up sending you?" Ren asked.

She told him about her father's farm in southwest Missouri and his desire to get away from the crime-ridden city.

"Were you happy there?" he asked.

"I suppose I was. I was much happier in college, though. David and I both studied journalism at Northwestern. Chicago is my home now. I love it there."

He smiled and sipped the green tea that their waiter had brought. "So, what brings you to California?"

"I'm trying to reconstruct my memory. I'm not having much luck. The first and only thing I have remembered is that you took me on the Santa Monica Ferris wheel once."

"Really? Well, that's something. We were close back then, so I'm flattered you remember it. How far back does your memory go?"

"I basically can't remember anything much before we moved to Missouri."

David spoke up. "We were here a month ago on a story, and she dragged me to Santa Monica. When she saw the Ferris wheel, she insisted we take a ride. When we reached the top, she remembered riding it once before. Until then, she didn't even have a clue she'd ever been to California before."

He looked into her face, his eyebrows drawn together in concern. "So, you really have amnesia, eh? Caused by the trauma of your kidnapping, I suppose. That was so horrible. I don't know how we all got through it."

"Yes. They call it psychogenic memory loss. I did go to the Mason clinic to try some therapy, but it was too traumatic. My therapist and I decided that hypnosis and even therapy would be too harmful to me."

His face still reflected concern. "So why are you here now, trying to do it on your own, if I may ask?"

She exchanged a look with David. Should they really get into this?

"Someone is trying to kill her," he said. "They don't know her memory is gone. We suppose it is someone who wasn't caught all those years ago."

Ren's eyebrows shot up. "Trying to kill Blythe! You can't be serious!"

"He is," Paula said.

"What do they hope to gain from that, I wonder?"

"We think someone who wasn't caught thinks I will recognize him. We were kind of hoping you could help us since you knew the family so well."

"I would be happy to do anything I can. Do you need a lawyer, then? I do mostly corporate work, but sometimes, like today, I handle personal matters for my clients. I also know the head of the FBI."

Paula interjected, "It's not exactly legal work we had in mind, and we're already working with the FBI. We were just wondering if you had any idea, from the time you spent with my parents during the kidnapping, of who specifically might be behind it."

"As you know," said David, "She was treated quite brutally. She still has the scars, inside and out. Was there anyone who had a personal vendetta against her parents?"

"You mean other than those who hated Chet for being a witness for the state and taking down one of the biggest drug rings in history?" He shook his head in wonder. "What an operator. He made a lot of enemies, but he is a law enforcement hero."

"I didn't realize it was that big," said Paula.

"It was huge. He did a masterful job."

"So, a lot of people really hated him," Paula said. "But did you get the feeling there was anyone who didn't get picked up? Anyone who might still be out there?"

"You mean a Mr. Big?"

"Right."

"I can't say that I did. I thought it was more of a syndicate, run by the guys who are now in that prison in Colorado. Except for your kidnappers. They're in Terre Haute, I understand."

This was so different from the view held by Fred, that Paula questioned him again, "So you don't think any one person was running it?"

"I never had that impression."

"Hmm. What did my father think?"

"You mean you never discussed it?" Ren's eyebrows went up in surprise.

"I never knew one thing about all this until after my father died when the FBI and Marshal Sutherland told me I was in WITSEC. Until after the marshal's death, I didn't even know why. My memories start in Missouri. If this person hadn't killed the marshal and tried to kill me, I would have thought that the whole thing was over and done with. Now, I know it isn't. Otherwise, why would they be trying to kill me?"

Their food arrived, but no one noticed.

"Someone miscalculated badly, then, didn't they?"

"And there's a rat in the FBI who's helping that someone to keep tabs on her," said David.

"I'll tell you what I'll do," said Ren. "If you subpoena the case files from the U.S. Attorney's office and get the court records, I'll go through them with a fine-toothed comb, looking for anything that wasn't followed up on or that might have been missed."

Paula thought a fresh pair of eyes might see something they and Fred might have missed. It was a very generous offer.

"Thank you so much," said Paula. "And if you could keep your ear to the ground, that would be much appreciated."

"Will do," Ren said.

She moved to scoop some Peking duck onto her plate. "Now, let's eat, and you can entertain us all by telling what a holy terror I was when I was a child."

He told stories about trips they took on his boat to Catalina and how brave she was out on the water and how she never got seasick. Talking about the time he took her and her mother to San Francisco, he said, "That's why I picked Shoots for our lunch today. I remember how much you loved Chinatown. Especially fortune cookies."

"How did we get to be such good friends?" she asked.

"Your mother and I grew up together on the wrong side of the tracks. We were boyfriend and girlfriend in those days. We both had a dream of getting out of Compton. We helped each other. Then she met your dad, and it was a love for the ages. I gave her up with bad grace, I'm afraid. But we continued to be friends. And then you came along, and I fell for you completely. You're the closest thing to a child I've ever had."

"Are you married now?"

"Not anymore. And she was a career woman with no desire for children. You can't imagine what a big day this is for me to see you all grown up."

The luncheon was delicious. Paula stuffed herself, but she noticed that David withdrew from the conversation more and more. Of course, that was understandable — he didn't really have a stake in it.

When they all parted in the foyer of the restaurant, she was smiling after Ren's departing back.

"That guy was in love with your mother, or I'm Mick Jagger."

"I know," she said with a sigh. "It kind of sticks out doesn't it? And I don't think he liked my father much, either."

She handed him her fortune from her cookie. It read, *Beware lying tongues around you.*

He laughed. "Well, at least he offered to help. That's a big job he offered to do," David said.

"And I have the feeling he's a very good lawyer."

"I grant you that."

CHAPTER TWENTY-FIVE

Paula thought a moment while they walked to the car. "You know, for sure there is an interview with my father in those papers we have. Probably many interviews. It would interest me to know what his opinion was on a 'Mr. Big.' Why would he have wanted to be in WITSEC if he didn't think our family was still in danger?"

"You're right, sweets. Even though we had that talk with Fred, and it is a daunting task, I still think we should go through them. Particularly if we're going to pass them on to Uncle Rennie."

They drove the short way to the FBI office and resumed their task looking through the U.S. Attorney's office's records.

Paula was the one who found the interviews with her father. They were clipped together and took place over the period of a week.

"Wow, this is going to be a big job," she said. "But, I think I need to read it, if only as a tribute to my dad. Two years of his life here."

"I'd offer to help," said David. "But I think one person needs to read the whole thing to get the complete picture."

"I agree," said Paula. "I'll take notes to summarize for you."

She began the task, but by five o'clock, she was still only halfway through. She decided to take the rest of the pages back to the B & B. She knew she wouldn't be able to sleep until she had gone through them. The risks her father had taken blew her mind. He sure did put his heart and soul into the case.

"My dad was good. Really good. And he certainly had the impression that the organization was run with more lead than silver. Everyone was afraid," she said on the way home to their B & B. "They started out being enticed by the money, which was generous, but once they were in there was no way out except death. Sounds like our last case."

"Yeah. I think these drug rings pretty much run true to type," David said. "By the way, while you were working on that, I talked to Moreno this afternoon. They did search Billy Porter's houses back in Chicago. He had a home in Lake Geneva and a condo on the

Gold Coast. They e-mailed me an inventory of the things they found. There's a couple of things I want to have a look at. They're going to FedEx them to me."

"Any leads on Porter?"

"They think he's left the country. No sign of him."

Neither of them had an appetite for dinner, so they went straight to the B & B, where Paula changed into yoga pants and a sweatshirt. David turned on the news, and they curled up together on one of the couches to watch it.

Halfway through there was an ad for Renwood Fullmer's campaign for Senate. Both Paula and David were interested to see that he was running his campaign on a law and order platform with a particular focus on ridding the state of the drug business. He showed himself to be quite passionate about it.

"When are you going to get the documents to him?" David asked.

"As soon as I've finished going over them," she said. "Speaking of which, I need to get back to them."

Reading the interviews of her father and all the evidence he had gathered brought her closer to him. She was very glad to know that he had been in touch with Agent Moreno about the drug traffic in southwest Missouri. She had thought he'd died a meth cook. Now, reading all the risks he'd taken earlier in his life to bring the drug traffickers to justice, she could see that he would never have done such a thing, even for her mother, if he hadn't been undercover. She was also very glad that she and David had finished that investigation, and that it was shut down forever.

When she neared the end of the interviews, Fred Almora had asked her father straight out if he thought there was a "Mr. Big."

Definitely. This organization is completely compartmentalized. The purchasers of the raw product are on one level, the packagers on another, and the distributors on another. They don't know each other. Someone has to be coordinating them. Also, there is transportation from one city to another. I don't think we have caught the main man.

He also takes a huge cut. The money from the sales is only partially accounted for. The rest goes to him. He is an exceedingly wealthy individual. He most certainly lives a double life. No one but his top generals know who he is, and they will not expose him, because that would mean death. Even in prison.

"Well, we have our answer," Paula said. She handed the transcript of the interview to David.

"Interesting. I guess he didn't talk much about the case to your mother's admirer. That doesn't surprise me."

"I don't think she was having an affair, David," she said. "My mother totally loved my father. And if you had known him in the days before my mother's illness, you would have understood why. He was larger than life. A John Wayne type. And he adored my mother. Her death left him with no desire to go on. He took chances he shouldn't have."

David said, "I didn't think she was. I think Fullmer's love was unrequited. I just got that feeling."

"I did, too. Poor man."

David came over to her and pulled her into his arms. "Have you really had a crush on me for five years?"

"I have. It was your voice I first fell for. Perfect broadcaster's voice. It just gathered me in and made me feel safe."

"I hope I can always make you feel that way. But our profession hasn't proved to be the safest thing in the world."

"Yeah, I know. But now that I've read these interviews, I can see that I'm my father's daughter, for sure."

* * *

When Paula woke up the next morning, she desperately wanted to go for a walk on the beach. Surely her FBI minder would take care of her, wouldn't he? But it wasn't fair to put him in danger for a whim on her part.

Instead, she assembled the documents she'd brought home, took a shower, got dressed and left for Joe's Café to have breakfast and bring David some biscuits and gravy.

CHAPTER TWENTY-SIX

David was dismayed to find that he had slept until ten o'clock. Worrying over the case, he hadn't been able to fall asleep until the wee hours. He had an uneasy feeling he couldn't identify. But going over the facts they knew hadn't led him anywhere.

A look around the studio showed that Paula wasn't there. Where did she go? Why hadn't she awakened him? Mumbling to himself, he headed for the shower. When he had finished, shaved, and dressed, she still hadn't returned.

He looked for a note, but all he found was the stack of documents Paula had brought home from the FBI office. He walked outside to find their minder sitting in his car across the street from the B & B.

He walked over to the guy and said, "Where's Paula? My partner?"

The minder said, "Another agent met her at that café for breakfast. They went off somewhere in his car."

"How do you know it was another agent?" he asked.

The guy was young. A sweat broke out on his upper lip. "I recognized him. It was Agent Forrest, the guy assigned to your case along with Agent Moreno."

David felt relief wash over him. "Did they say where they were going?"

"No. They didn't even look my way. I think they forgot I was even there."

"That's weird."

"Yeah. A little. But they were real friendly with each other. He wasn't forcing her or anything."

David went across to Joe's Café where he ordered coffee, an omelet, and an order of biscuits and gravy. Then he called Paula, which is what he should have done in the first place.

Her phone went immediately to voice mail. He had watched her plug it in to charge the night before. His earlier anxiety returned. Drinking his coffee absently, he finally decided to call Agent Moreno.

"Have you seen your partner this morning?" he asked when Moreno picked up.

"He's not in today. Migraine. He has a history of them."

David's heart almost stopped. "Wrong. He's got Paula. Stole her right out of the diner this morning."

"What in the world are you talking about?"

David's jaw was tight as he ground his teeth. "The man you have guarding us saw them. They walked out of the café together and now I can't raise her on her phone."

There was a beat of silence. Then, "I'll try to call him and get right back to you."

David looked at the breakfast the waitress was setting before him, then looked up at her. "Did you see my partner come in this morning? We usually come in together? She has blonde hair? Hazel eyes?"

"Yeah. I saw her. She was with another dude. It was around eight o'clock. They were real friendly. Left together. He paid for her breakfast."

"Listen, this is important. Did you hear anything they said?"

"Sure. They didn't notice me. Some people are like that, y'know? He said he came to pick her up, but that she could eat her breakfast first. She was wanted down at some kind of headquarters."

"Thanks." David gave her a twenty as he stood up. "Keep the change. I don't have time to eat."

His phone rang. Moreno. "What d'ya got?" David asked.

"Forrest didn't answer. I left a voicemail."

"Good for you. I just found out from the waitress that he said he was taking her into headquarters. That was over two and a half hours ago. The FBI minder just watched them walk away."

"You think Forrest is bent. You think he kidnapped Ms. James."

"Do you have another explanation?" David was doing all he could to hang on to his temper. This wasn't Moreno's fault.

"I'll meet you at his place. Apartment 12, 2158 Gardenia Street, Costa Mesa. You got GPS?"

"Yeah. I'm on my way."

As he drove, he thought of all the things that should have tipped him off. He had known someone concerned in the case was dirty. Someone had arranged to get Billy Porter out of jail. And someone with nefarious intentions had shown up in Minnesota. Only two people knew they were going to the clinic. Agents Moreno and Forrest. David had thought maybe the agents had communicated with someone higher up, and the word had gotten out that way. But no. It was way simpler than that. Forrest himself had been in touch with Porter.

Who were Billy Porter and Forrest working for? The Main Bad Guy as Paula called him? Probably, yes. David now knew that the MBG had a Chicago operation. Porter wasn't just a hired killer. He was connected to the MBG here in California through his organization.

Forrest was too young to have been concerned with Paula's father's case. He must have been turned in the last few years.

But Paula. *Oh, Lord, help.*

He drove like a maniac through the congestion, raising honking horns and obscene gestures. When he reached the apartment building, Moreno was there before him, standing outside the door. David ran up the stairs.

"No answer, I take it?" he asked.

"Right."

David said, "Turn around. You didn't see this." Using the picklock on his key chain, David unlocked and opened the door.

The apartment was neat as a pin and completely empty. There wasn't so much as an errant whisker in the bathroom sink. The closets were empty. The shelves were empty. The beds were stripped, the sheets gone.

"This place smells like bleach," said Moreno. "It's been totally wiped down."

"He's gone over to the dark side, that's for sure."

"He's a sleeper." Moreno grimaced. "Whatever the reason for kidnapping Paula, it must be huge for them to bring him in when he's been in place for three years."

"Yeah," said David. "I think it means we're getting too close for Mr. Big's peace of mind."

Depression settled over him, thinking of the urban sprawl that was LA and Orange Counties. "She could be anywhere," he said.

"Forrest's prints are in the system. I'm going to cross-reference them with IAFIS," said Moreno. "Maybe that wasn't done when he was at Quantico."

"We also need to go over all the paperwork on him—his background check, everything. There may be a clue there."

"I'll meet you back at headquarters," said Moreno.

* * *

The FBI headquarters in D.C. had to be approached by the Special Agent in Charge of the Orange County office. It was two o'clock before the faxes arrived with Forrest's personal information, application, and prints.

David was almost literally pulling out his hair by that time.

Paula. Dear Lord, Paula. Where is she? What are they doing to her? Have they killed her?

While waiting for the documents from D.C., David put together a news release.

Ms. Paula James, also known as Blythe Kensington, a noted television journalist from Chicago, has been reported missing. It is believed she was forcibly abducted by the man known as Edward Forrest, who had been posing as an FBI agent out of Orange County for the past three years.

Ms. James is five feet seven inches tall with blonde hair and hazel eyes. An investigative journalist, she has recently been seen on television in connection with the bust of a worldwide methamphetamine ring, headquartered in Bentonville, Arkansas and run by notorious Irish gang boss, Magnus O'Toole.

Forrest is five feet, nine inches tall, of muscular build. His hair is blond and receding. He has blue eyes and a tanned complexion.

David had a color publicity photo of Paula sent to him over email from WOOT. Moreno got him a headshot of Forrest from FBI files. When everything was completed, David called KTLA, KCBS, WOOT, Fox News, and CNN, telling them he was emailing them the news release and asking for their help in airing it that evening as often as possible.

By the time he had done that, the details on Forrest had been faxed through from D.C. Moreno called a meeting of all the agents in the office and put everything up on the big screen in the conference room.

Forrest had claimed to have been raised in Prosperity, South Carolina by a single mother. He was a quiet but exemplary student. He won a scholarship to Duke where he majored in Political Science. He played baseball for the university but wasn't good enough to qualify for the MLB draft.

There were three recommendations from professors at the university which had been verified. They all praised his brilliance and his desire to raise himself from his humble origins. He had been a member of the student senate and had participated in the moot court competition. His grades yielded a 3.87 average.

He won the coveted MacMillan Award for Citizenship, which carried a scholarship to be applied to tuition at the law school of his choice. Scoring very high on the LSAT, he had been accepted at Duke University School of Law.

Even with the scholarship, he had found himself unable to continue after his first year, because of financial considerations. He needed to go to work to take care of his mother who was ill and had no income.

It was at this point that he had applied at the FBI and was accepted.

His background check at Duke and in Prosperity had uncovered no affiliations with anti-American or criminal associates of any kind.

"It was the money," said Moreno. "That was his vulnerable spot."

"You can take the boy out of Prosperity, but apparently you can't take Prosperity out of the boy," said the SAC. "I wouldn't be surprised to find out that he got his start as a drug operator while he was in college, or during that year in law school. The organization would have loved having someone in the FBI. What has happened to the mother?"

"Look up the address in Prosperity on Google Maps," said David.

The map appeared on the screen showing the address to be a trailer park. They went back over his background checks, but there was no mention of a mother. Moreno called the owner of the trailer park. Mrs. Forrest had moved away three years ago. No. He had no forwarding address. Obviously, at the time Forrest joined the FBI, he had come into enough money to move his mother out of Prosperity.

Surrounded by chatter the next twenty minutes, David went over everything he knew about the case.

Who did they know who had enough money to tempt Forrest to work for him? How had a kid from Duke become involved with the drug rings they were investigating? Did they have a wider outreach than they had previously thought? Had he joined up with the organization before or after he joined the FBI? Forrest was close to the top of the organization. How had he risen so fast? Was anyone else at the FBI involved?

Who was threatened by the secrets Paula didn't know she was keeping? Someone with a heck of a lot to lose. Someone with a very public profile.

The problem was, this wasn't Chicago, and David didn't know the players. Who was who in California? In Orange County? Maybe Renwood Fullmer would have some ideas. He would like to inform him of Paula's kidnapping anyway. Maybe he could help.

He ran the idea by Moreno and told him he was going to Fullmer's office for a visit.

"Good. We can use all the insight we can get."

CHAPTER TWENTY-SEVEN

"Why didn't Uncle Rennie get in touch with me himself?" asked Paula over her bowl of oatmeal. "Oh, I forgot. I didn't give him my contact information."

"He came into headquarters yesterday afternoon after a court case. Asked if we knew how to get in touch with you. He's got some ideas to bounce off you. Some stuff he remembered. I really didn't want to give out that info without your okay, so I told him I'd bring you down to headquarters this morning to meet with him."

"Why didn't you just call me?" she asked. "Or did you just want an excuse to eat at Joe's? They have biscuits and gravy to die for, David says."

"Right out of my childhood. You got it. I'm a southern boy." He proceeded to order biscuits and gravy. "Truth is, I didn't have your new cell number. Agent Burrows over there told me this is where you eat breakfast. Did you know this is a Pacific Coast icon?"

"So I understand. Even their oatmeal is special. Creamy like you wouldn't believe."

"Our appointment is at ten-thirty. The traffic from here to Santa Ana isn't too bad. Worse going the other direction."

When they had finished eating, they left the restaurant.

"This doesn't look like an FBI issued car!" she said, eying a black Mustang convertible with the top down.

"Agent Moreno has our car this morning. I thought I could just run you in using my car. Thought you might like to see the beach from a convertible. Nothing beats it."

Paula began to suspect that the agent might be trying to impress her. How could he *not* have noticed that she and David were together?

A traffic accident lengthened the ride to Santa Ana. As they sat in traffic, she asked, "You say you're a southern boy. Where are you from?"

"Little town in South Carolina. Went to Duke. Then I decided to join the Bureau. They sent me out here, and I can't say I'm sorry. I like Orange County."

"I think I grew up here, but you already know I can't remember."

"Must be a bummer."

"Yeah."

When they reached Santa Ana, they ventured into a ghetto-like area she'd never seen before. Her instincts prickled. "This isn't where headquarters is."

"I just have to run in and pay my cleaning lady. I forgot to leave her money out yesterday. I told her I'd bring it by this morning. There's plenty of time."

She watched as he walked up to the door and knocked.

Something hard hit the back of her head. That was the last thing she knew before the world went black.

CHAPTER TWENTY-EIGHT

David was waiting, trying to master his impatience as he sat in Oakley, Howell, and Fullmer's waiting room. Mr. Fullmer wanted to see him, but he was with a client.

Standing, David walked over to the side of the room that was floor to ceiling glass. He clenched his fists in his pockets. Then he began pacing the room. He noticed for the first time the framed photos on the wall of Fullmer shaking hands and posing with important looking people. There was even a sculpture on the coffee table that proved to be an award he had received from Hoag Hospital in Newport Beach as Donor of the Year. A bound book of news clippings sat next to it. David perused it and was impressed to see that Renwood Fuller had donated money for a new wing to be built at Hoag Hospital for experimental research on breast cancer. Other clippings showed him receiving the legal pro bono award for representing a school for the disabled in a case in Santa Ana.

He went back to the ocean view. It was endless; the horizon smudged a bit by the marine haze. It made him feel hopeless. Where in the world had they taken Paula? She could be anywhere. He hadn't the slightest idea where to look.

Was she already dead? He couldn't fathom that possibility, but he suddenly felt so useless, he had to sit down again. What was he going to tell Fullmer?

At last a woman in a black sheath and stiletto heels came to tell him Mr. Fullmer would see him.

As he walked into the spacious office with its view of the sea, he was suddenly ill.

"She's gone," he said, his voice flat. "Paula, Blythe, whatever you call her. She was kidnapped this morning. I thought you would want to know."

The man leaped to his feet. "Blythe? Kidnapped? But that's outrageous! No," he growled. "That can't be. I just found her again after all these years. What is being done?"

"The FBI is working on it. We know who did it. A dirty FBI agent named Forrest. But we assume he was working for someone else, and we don't know who that is. We have no idea where she's being held or even if she's alive."

"Have you found this Forrest fellow?"

"No. But we have a BOLO out for him, and we're putting it out on the evening news."

"That's not enough. That poor girl shouldn't have to go through this again. I'm putting a call in to the boss over there. She knows me."

David thought this couldn't hurt, and listened to Fullmer put a call straight through to the Special Agent in Charge. He blustered, he postured, he threatened. Hoping Moreno wasn't going to be called on the carpet, David began to wonder if it had been such a great idea to come over here.

"Have you called the *Orange County Register* and *Los Angeles Times*?" asked Fullmer. "They can have the information up on their online edition in minutes."

"That's a good idea," David said. "I can see I did the right thing coming to you. Paula was still working on her kidnapping case. Do you know anyone prominent who might be dirty enough to have engineered all this? Someone with something to hide?"

Fullmer came out from behind the desk and began pacing on the Persian rug, hands behind his back.

"I always thought that was Herrera, myself."

"Who is Herrera?"

"A Colombian drug lord. Ruthless. Everywhere he goes, he leaves death in his wake."

"But what would he have to lose by being exposed in this country? He can hide in Colombia."

"It has his stamp on it. He is unnecessarily cruel." Fullmer chopped the side of his hand as though it were the blade of a guillotine.

"We know that whoever was at the head of that drug operation that Paula's father brought down wasn't caught," said David. "We know he still has operations in the mountain west and Chicago."

He saw the man nod his head, but he said nothing.

"Herrera," he repeated. "I feel it. You go find that Forrest fellow, and I'll call my friends at the DEA."

David took this as his dismissal.

"This has bowled me over," Fullmer said as David took out one of his business cards. He wrote his phone number on the back of it and left it on the corner of the desk. "Let me know if you think of anything."

* * *

David traveled back to the odd town of Santa Ana. He wondered how all the people in the ghettoish town could afford Orange County housing prices. When he reached the FBI building, he suddenly remembered the FedEx package he was due to receive that day from Chicago. It would be here by now. He could use the distraction.

Agent Moreno's face was tense, and the lines around his mouth looked deeper. "I can't believe I didn't see that my partner was bent," he said to David. "I know I'm sorry doesn't cut it, but I *am* sorry. How did your visit go with Fullmer?"

"He called your boss. When I left, he was calling the DEA. He's convinced someone called Herrara is behind this. I don't see it myself," David said with a heavy sigh. "Tell me my FedEx package arrived."

"It did. It's on one of those desks you and Paula were using."

"Thanks."

A package the size of a shoebox sat on Paula's desk. He opened it without much expectation. It had several manila envelopes inside. The first one was labeled: Gold Coast condo.

Inside were photos of all the rooms. The man apparently loved to hunt. There were trophies mounted on the walls, including a 12-point elk head. Also, an arsenal of hunting weapons festooned the walls. In a smaller envelope was an accounting book. It appeared to be in code. Or maybe it was the key to a code. He had no idea. There were people in the FBI that specialized in that sort of thing. David would have to be certain they had received a copy.

The next large envelope was labeled: Lake Geneva property. There were letters in there that appeared to be written in the code that corresponded with the book.

David couldn't wait. He picked up the desk phone and dialed Moreno. "Could you come here a minute? I have something to show you."

Moreno seized on the codes with enthusiasm. "No need to send these to Quantico just yet. Let me work on them. I had special training in codes. I worked in that department for a while."

There was one more, smaller envelope. Inside were pictures. Snapshots. David peered at them closely. These were hunting photos as well, but they weren't taken in the US. There were elephants. Even a lion.

Porter must have taken an illegal safari. The last photo was of a group of men—presumably other members of the group. Before them, on the ground was a dead elephant. Two men appeared to be sawing off its tusks.

There. Standing in the back row was a man with an old-fashioned colonial pith helmet. Smiling at the camera was Renwood Fullmer.

CHAPTER TWENTY-NINE

Paula came to her senses in a dark room that smelled like salsa. Her head throbbed, and she couldn't see the slightest bit of light. When she realized her hands and feet were tied, she fought off impending panic.

She knew from her nightmares what had happened when her hands and feet had been tied and when it had been dark. What was going to happen now? How did she even get here?

Her already fractured memory was not working. The last thing she remembered was going to bed. Had it been last night? She had no sense of time.

But she did have her hearing. Paula heard a heated argument, but she couldn't understand the words. Spanish, maybe? To go with the salsa?

Her eyes were heavy, and she fought sleep.

I need to stay awake. To be ready.

Ready for what? Maybe it would be better if I got just a little more sleep. Maybe my head will feel better when I wake up.

The next time she woke up she felt thirsty. Horribly thirsty. Just like she had been when she was in the mountain cabin, and those awful men wouldn't give her any water. Or food.

Right now, she didn't feel like eating. She was too nauseous.

It had seemed like the time in the mountain cabin would never end. She had lain in a dark room like this one for days in terrific pain. Her left arm and her left leg hurt so badly she could barely stand it. And she was so thirsty.

There had been only mean and nasty men there. She had known they didn't have any children. They wouldn't have treated her that way if they had.

All at once she realized she might not remember how she got here, but she remembered those horrible days of her captivity when she was a child. The horrible episode of her life was coming back to her.

CHAPTER THIRTY

So. Fullmer had been on an illegal safari with a professional assassin. Could Fullmer himself be the arch villain? The idea made David sick. At one time in her life, Paula had worshipped the man.

But this picture more or less clinched the deal that he was a bad guy, despite all his good works. "Uncle Rennie" wouldn't want the voting public to know he was friends with an assassin and had killed an elephant.

Agent Moreno came back to David's desk.

"This is kind of a disappointment," he said, indicating the codebook. "It is too easy. Just a number substitution code. But the contents are hot stuff."

"Anything that will help?"

"He was blackmailing Forrest. Knew he was a crooked agent."

"What else? Anything about Fullmer?"

"Why do you ask that?"

David showed him the safari snapshot. "They knew each other. They went on an illegal safari together. But, I think it more likely that Billy Porter works for Fullmer. He probably ran the Chicago organization if they recreated together. This is sort of a bad guy's version of golf."

"Hah!" said Moreno.

"I told him you had a BOLO out on Forrest."

"Yes. It is also on the 5:00 and 6:00 news with a photo and description of his car. And we're watching the airports. So far nothing. What if he moved his mother out here and he's gone home to Mommy?"

David wanted to put a fist through a wall. Instead, he kicked his chair. "I hate this place. It's teeming with people. In Chicago, the gangs hang out together in neighborhoods. You know where to find them, at least."

"Forrest has a distinctive car," said Moreno. "A black 2018 Mustang convertible. I don't think he would part with it for anything. I've put a separate BOLO out on it."

Moreno's phone rang.

David heard him say, "We'll be right there."

"Forrest, I think. Body matching his description found on a boat registered to him in Balboa Bay Harbor. Police called by the owner of the boat in the next slip. They saw his FBI creds."

"So, he had a boat and a Mustang, and you didn't think that was strange on his salary?"

"I didn't know about the boat. That car was something he said he'd saved for over a period of years."

They drove down to Newport in the FBI black Chevy Impala. The sight of all the beautiful boats moored in the harbor would have taken David's breath away under other circumstances. Now his eyes locked on the police cruiser parked along one of the narrow streets on Balboa Island. "What'll you wanna bet Fullmer is behind this?" he asked.

"You're probably right. Didn't want him talking to us."

Parking places were apparently at a premium here, and they had to double park. He and Moreno walked up to the sergeant who awaited them at the end of a pier.

"Sergeant Hinshaw," he stuck out his hand to Moreno and shook.

"Special agent Moreno. This is David van Pelt from Chicago. His partner was kidnapped by Forrest this morning. Any sign of her on the boat?"

"Nothing that we saw. My lieutenant is still on it. Let's go."

Forrest had owned a large sailboat, even by Newport Beach standards. All its sails were wrapped up tight and snapped down under royal blue canvas. As they stepped on board, David saw Forrest's body, right in the middle of the teak-planked deck, a bullet hole through his forehead.

"There are signs of a struggle inside. He appears to have been dragged out here post-mortem," said a short, compact man who introduced himself as Lieutenant Kramar.

"Anybody hear the shot or see anything?"

"Not so far as we have been able to determine. We think a suppressor must have been used, close as these boats and houses are together."

"How long has he been dead?" asked David, as fears for Paula raged through him.

"Only an hour or so, at an estimate. Our ME is on the way."

As Moreno looked down at his former partner, David could read the sadness on his face. "I should have known something was wrong before it came to this."

"Someone didn't want him to talk," said David.

"This is a crime scene, so you had better stay here, while I go down inside and see what I can see," the agent said.

David asked the Lieutenant, "Who found him?"

"Guy in the next boat over. He'd just arrived to take out his boat. As you can see, it sits higher. He looked right down onto the deck."

"Did he know Forrest?"

"He knew him as Dan Andrews. He passed himself off as a wealthy retired guy. He was here a lot."

David's energy ebbed lower, and he sat on a bench along the railing. With Forrest dead, was there any chance of finding Paula alive?

CHAPTER THIRTY-ONE

*U*ncle Rennie. His face had been there in her dream. *Impossible.* If he had been in the mountain cabin, he would have rescued her. Wouldn't he? How could he have had anything to do with her kidnapping? She was getting the two cases confused. She'd seen Uncle Rennie yesterday, not all those years ago. Not in the mountain cabin. But her dream had confused her. He told the men who held her that they had done a good job, except that they needed to give her more water or she was going to die on them. If she died, they wouldn't have any "leverage."

She hadn't known what leverage was, but it must have been a magic word, for suddenly they supplied her with a whole case of bottled water in addition to freeing her hands so that she could get to it.

"Uncle Rennie, can't you take me home?" she had asked.

Then she had awakened to this horrible place. Would whoever was holding her kill her this time?

If only she had her Glock. But it was all right. Somehow she would make do. She wasn't nine years old anymore. And she had taken down a drug empire once. She could do it again.

Oh, David. Dear David. I know you would have saved me from this if you could. Don't blame yourself.

Would she ever have gone on national TV if she had known what was at risk if she were recognized? Why had her parents kept the secret of who they really were? She could understand why they would when she was young, but what about after she became an adult?

Paula froze as she heard two sets of heavy footsteps coming to this part of the house. Was this the end, then? Would she be silenced for good?

CHAPTER THIRTY-TWO

As they were headed back to where they'd double parked, Moreno's phone rang once more. Part way through the recital on the other end, he gave David a thumbs-up. Hope surged inside of him.

"On our way, thanks for the good work."

"The car was spotted in a crummy neighborhood in Santa Ana this morning by a curious neighbor who watched the 5 o'clock news. She called the TV station who called our tips line. I've got the address."

"Don't you have a siren on this thing?" David said.

CHAPTER THIRTY-THREE

"Uncle Rennie," she said, echoing her dream as the man walked into the room and turned on the light. "Have you come to rescue me?"

"You can lose the act," he said, his voice flat.

A sense of betrayal assailed her, so deep it nearly sank her. *It wasn't a dream. He had been in the mountain cabin all those years ago. And he knew she had seen him.*

"Of course you haven't," she said. "You betrayed an innocent little girl. Broke her heart."

"I knew you would remember. But it was all your mother's doing. You can blame her." Ren Fullmer's handsome face grew ugly.

"My mother had nothing to do with it," said Paula.

"She turned her back on me. She chose *him. A lowly cop.*"

"Instead of you. A wealthy drug lord."

"I had loved her since we were kids. I did it all for her," he said. "And then she turned her back on me."

"You're poison. Why do you think she couldn't see that?"

"You didn't. You loved me."

"Why did you treat me so cruelly?" she demanded. "I all but worshipped you. I hardly knew my father back then."

"Revenge," he said simply. "I wanted her to suffer like she'd made me suffer."

"You're abominable. A real sociopath." She put every ounce of disdain she could summon into her voice.

"Give her the needle, Billy," Ren Fullmer said.

For the first time, Paula focused on his companion. "Billy Porter," she said. "Your pet killer."

Porter opened the case in his hands and took out a hypodermic syringe. Feeling maddeningly helpless, she watched as he approached her, grabbed her arm, and jabbed her with the needle.

CHAPTER THIRTY-FOUR

"**H**is vanity was his downfall," said Agent Moreno as they drove towards the street in Santa Ana where the Mustang had been seen.

"Looks like," said David. "Do you speak Spanish?"

"My mother tongue," said Moreno.

As they turned the corner, they spotted the house number. It belonged to a small pistachio-colored stucco bungalow with a crumbling walk. All the blinds were drawn. Parking a few houses away, they approached the house from the side. Moreno had brought in back-up in a car that now parked behind theirs. All four agents drew their guns. Two went around back. While Moreno knocked on the door, his remaining backup agents stood each to one side of him, backs flush with the house. David stood to the side as well.

No one answered the door. Moreno put on gloves and tried the knob.

"Locked," he said. "We have probable cause to break the door down. Paula may be being kept here against her will and is in physical danger. Her life has been threatened several times." He explained all this to his backup team.

"Going in," said one of the agents into his radio.

The agents used a heavy steel battering ram on the door until it finally gave way. David wanted to run in, but he restrained himself while the agents cleared the rooms one by one. Finally, he heard, "Clear. Victim is in the bedroom. No one else is on the premises."

David ran in to see Paula as Moreno got on his phone to call for an ambulance. She lay huddled on the bare floor. He spoke to her, but she didn't respond. Panicked, he rolled her over and checked a pulse. He found a faint one that was alarmingly slow.

She had most probably been drugged. He prayed it hadn't been a fatal dose. Chaffing her hands, he sat cross-legged on the dirty floor, her head in his lap, waiting for help to arrive. He stroked her cheek.

"Oh, honey. You've got to come around. Please don't tell me we got here too late."

The sirens blared from somewhere close by. As they neared, he kissed Paula's cheek. "Please, God," he whispered. "Let her live."

In moments the paramedics filled the room.

"I suspect someone gave her an overdose. Probably heroin. Her pulse is really faint," the EMT said.

One of the paramedics took a small canister out of his kit.

"Naloxone," he said briefly. After removing the cap, he put the canister up to Paula's nose and sprayed its contents into her left nostril.

"If we're in time, that should neutralize the heroin or any other opioid she may have ingested. But we need to take her with us into the hospital."

"I'm riding with you," he said. "Which hospital?"

"Orange County Global Medical Center," the first responder said.

Leaving Paula for a moment, he got up and raced to Moreno who was speaking with his back up about securing the scene. "I'm going to the hospital with Paula. Orange County Global. Hopefully, we got here in time. Looks like it was a drug overdose."

Moreno nodded. "We'll take it from here."

As they rode in the ambulance, siren screeching, David held Paula's hand. It seemed that they had spent entirely too much time in hospitals this last month. This time, however, it was Paula who was near death. Bending down, he kissed her forehead.

Please, God, let her live. I promise I'll take better care of her. She's my everything. I can't bear to lose her.

Did someone really think we would believe she did this herself?

Maybe Uncle Rennie thought he was being merciful.

When they reached the hospital, the paramedics transferred her to a gurney and Paula was whisked away from him. He wasn't a family member.

"You'll have to wait in the ER waiting room, sir," they told him.

* * *

He had read the ancient *Time* magazines from cover to cover. At least, his eyes had scanned the words. David couldn't have told anyone a single item from either periodical.

Finally, Moreno had joined him.

"We printed the house. Prints are being run on IAFIS. Got some dirty drinking glasses in the kitchen that may have DNA. How is she doing?"

"I'm trying to be hopeful. Don't you think they would have told me if she'd died?"

"Probably. This is tough, man."

"Any word on Forrest?"

"No one saw or heard anything until his body appeared on the boat deck. That was some boat."

"Yeah. I'm glad you don't have to prosecute him. That wouldn't have felt too good."

"I can't say I really ever liked the guy. I always thought he was too buttoned up. Shows what I know."

CHAPTER THIRTY-FIVE

Paula felt as though she were in a box with the lid slammed down and locked. She couldn't get out. *Might as well sleep.*

The next time she was aware, something inside her told her she should wake up; that it was important. How long had she been asleep anyway? And she was freezing. There were voices. How had an intercom gotten into her bedroom? Before she could contemplate this, the blackness enshrouded her again.

Then she heard them saying. "Maybe we were just too late. Maybe she's comatose."

She struggled to open her eyes, but it felt like her eyelids had weights on them. She wanted to move her hand. Anything. But she couldn't move.

Paula knew she wasn't comatose. At least, she hoped she wasn't. What did it feel like to be in a coma?

"There! I think her eyelashes moved!"

She recognized David's voice.

Trying to speak, she succeeded in moving her tounge, but not her mouth. She went back to trying to open her eyes. She partially succeeded, but then they dropped closed again.

"Yes!" David cried. "She's trying to open her eyes! She's in there. Paula! Paula! It's David. You're alive. You're here with us in the hospital."

She blinked again. He kissed her forehead. "Come on now. You can do it. Open those beautiful eyes."

Finally she managed to pry them open. Her surroundings looked unfamiliar, but David didn't. He was leaning over her, jubilant.

"You did it! You made it!"

She still couldn't speak, but she managed a little twitch of her lips. Looking around her gave her a headache. There was a white curtain pulled around her bed. An IV in her arm. She was in the hospital.

The injection that had been meant to kill her.

How had she survived?

Paula was so tired; she closed her eyes just as the curtain was pulled back. With great difficulty, she opened them again. A nurse in purple scrubs stood there.

"You're awake! We were beginning to think we'd lost you, but David here wouldn't give up."

He said, "You just came back from an opiate overdose. They gave you something to reverse it. I knew you'd make it! I tried to tell them you're Wonder Woman." He clasped her cold hand. "I knew you'd come back to me."

She wanted to talk, to tell the nurse she didn't take it herself, but her mouth wouldn't open. Trying to signal with her eyes, she looked at the IV.

The nurse said, "Saline. We're using it to clean the opiates out of your system. There is also a huge bump on the back of your head which we need to take care of. But you're awake, and that's the main thing."

She managed to nod her head slightly.

"Thank the Lord we got to you in time!" David said.

Agent Moreno entered. "Glad you're awake," he said. "Good job."

She was able to smile. David leaned down and kissed her on the forehead again.

"Agent Forrest was found shot to death," said Moreno. "Someone didn't want him talking if we managed to catch him. But he didn't do this to you, did he?"

Agent Forrest. Memories of that morning sailed into her head. Paula managed to wet her lips, but still couldn't speak. She had no idea what had happened to Agent Forrest. She just remembered sitting in his Mustang while he went to pay his cleaning lady. If only she could speak!

David said, "We found you late this afternoon in a rundown house in Santa Ana. We called the EMT's and they gave you the antidote or whatever it was about an hour ago. They said if you hadn't been out too long that it would work. Did Forrest leave you in the house or did he stay with you?"

She tried to remember, but couldn't. Tears welled in her eyes.

"Don't cry, sweets. You'll remember."

She blinked away the tears.

"You might be interested to know that we found a connection between Billy Porter and your friend Uncle Rennie. They went to Africa to kill elephants together."

A memory slammed into her head. Uncle Rennie. Billy Porter. She winced.

"What is it, sweets? Something about Uncle Rennie?"

She gave an exhausted nod.

He had been there in the cabin in the mountains. In the house today. Or was she confusing one with another?

"He's a bad guy if he hangs out with Billy Porter."

She nodded again. Billy Porter. He was definitely in the house today. She could picture him leaning over as he gave her a shot.

"He's the one that did this to you?"

She gave a little nod.

David began chaffing her hand. "I'll bring him in if it's the last thing I do," he said. "He's probably acting for Uncle Rennie."

Moreno said, "We've got FBI agents here to watch over you."

The nurse stepped in. "You gentlemen will have to leave now. She's recovering nicely, but she's going down to x-ray. Got to see if there's a skull fracture."

David kissed her again, this time on the lips and then he was gone. Paula's reactions may be slow, but his kiss had solved her temperature problem. She was warmed down to her toes.

It was during the x-ray that the memories started coming back. Uncle Rennie taunting her in that horrible room that smelled of salsa. Saying awful things about her mother and her father. He had kidnapped her out of revenge because her mother rejected him.

When she got back to her cubicle, the nurse let David know he could come back in.

He arrived and she was finally able to get out one word, "Ren."

"He was there?" David guessed. "He had Porter give you the heroin?"

She nodded.

He gave her a hug that pulled her up out of the bed.

"Go," she said.

CHAPTER THIRTY-SIX

There was a party going on at the Fullmer mansion in Big Canyon. The neo-Tuscan villa was lit up like Christmas. There was a string orchestra playing and what seemed like hundreds of people socializing.

David and Agent Moreno walked right in. This was going to be sweet. The crowd was dressed to the nines—men in white ties, women in long evening gowns. Champagne circulated on the trays of black-coated waiters.

David pulled out his phone, turned it to video, and stuck it in his shirt pocket with the lens trained on the crowd. A dais constructed at one end of the large room held the quartet of string players. As they watched, Renwood Fullmer climbed up to the platform and signaled the orchestra to take a break. He faced the crowd.

"I want to thank you all for coming and contributing so generously to my campaign . . . "

David focused his camera on Renwood Fullmer, archvillain, as FBI Agent Moreno climbed the steps to the dais.

"This is going to be a wonderful year," Fullmer continued. "Because of your support . . ."

He stopped his speech and looked inquiringly at Agent Moreno as he approached him. The FBI agent was clearly relishing his task as he removed handcuffs from an inner pocket and used them to cuff the stunned senatorial candidate.

"FBI," he said. "Renwood Fullmer, I am arresting you for the attempted murder of Paula James, also known as Blythe Kensington. You have the right to remain silent. Anything you say can and will be used against you in a court of law. You have the right to an attorney. If you cannot afford an attorney, one will be provided for you."

The crowd gasped, and in the wake of dead silence, Agent Moreno put his hand on Fullmer's bicep and attempted to escort him off the dais.

"You can't arrest me! I'm going to be elected to the U.S. Senate. I know your boss! I'll have your badge! I'll have you arrested for harassment! Frank? Where are you?"

All at once the crowd burst into fevered speech. Another man leaped up onto the dais. "Agent, by what right do you arrest my client?"

"Every right. The woman to whom he administered a lethal dose of opioids today was rescued and has survived. She named him as her assailant. We have every reason to believe her. That is all I am required to tell you."

Fullmer's ashen face looked pinched. "I am going to be the next senator from the State of California."

Moreno said. "Believe me, buddy, all that's over with and this is just the beginning."

The FBI agent's backup climbed the stairs, stepped around the lawyer, and strong-armed Renwood Fullmer off his stage.

David got it all with his phone.

There was a commotion as someone tried to run through the crowd. David wrenched his gaze from the platform and looked over his shoulder. Someone was making a break for the back of the house.

Without further thought, David gave chase. He was just in time to watch the runner push aside a waitress with a tray of canapes and attempt escape through the kitchen door. David passed the startled woman and followed the would-be escapee. He had hopped over the low wall and was running down the hill toward the golf course. He was fast. But David, fueled by the image of Paula's anguished face and by his own adrenaline caught up with him and slammed him to the ground.

To his deep satisfaction, he recognized the face of Billy Porter. "Ah, Mr. Porter! Don't you know it's bad luck to shoot elephants?"

Porter cursed.

An FBI agent had followed him and joined him at the scene.

"Got another pair of cuffs?" David asked. "We've got Mr. Billy Porter here. More attempted murder. Of me. A couple of weeks ago."

CHAPTER THIRTY-SEVEN

It was one a.m. when David finally came into Paula's hospital room. He had intended to just sit by her bed, but she was awake and had finally recovered her speech.

"David! Oh, David! Did you get them?"

"Yes, and the act was witnessed by California's social elite as they were wining and dining at Uncle Rennie's expense. I think we can safely say it was the social event of the season."

He pulled her up out of her bed into a thorough embrace. "I love you, Paula-Blythe James-Kensington. Thank you for coming back to me."

She hugged him back. "So they're both under arrest? Wait? You love me?"

"Of course I love you! How could you possibly doubt it?"

She responded to his question by giving him a deep kiss on the mouth.

"When can I get you out of here?"

"They want to keep me for twenty-four hours for observation. They think I'm fine now, but it was a near thing, and they want to make sure my organs are all recovered. They're doing tests," she said.

He sat down on the edge of her bed, and she smiled at him. "Tell me how you found me. I think it must have been just in time."

"We had a BOLO out for Forrest's car. We put it on the evening news. The neighbor remembered seeing it that morning. We stormed the house."

"I remembered," said Paula. "Renwood Fullmer was my kidnapper all those years ago. He betrayed my trust. He did it all out of anger toward my mother for choosing my father over him."

"How are you with that?"

"Pretty shaky. He came there tonight and clearly showed his sociopathic side. Then he had his dude, Porter, shoot me full of something to kill me, I guess."

"Heroin," said David. "I thought I'd lost you. But we got there just in time. The EMT's shot you full of something called Naloxone. I guess it did the trick. How are you feeling now, honey?"

"Like a sack of cement, but better than I did. So . . . I don't know what to call him . . . Fullmer, I guess. Will Fullmer be indicted on charges related to all his drug rings, too?"

"Yup. Now that his boss is in solitary in the jail in Santa Ana and can't order his death, Billy Porter is singing like a bird. He wants a plea deal. He was his number two man these last few years. We may get testimony from those guys already in prison, too, now that we've got Fullmer."

She listened as he told her the very satisfactory story of Fullmer's arrest.

"That was justice on a grand scale!" she said, managing a laugh. "What happened to Agent Forrest?"

"We'll probably never know his whole story. We found him shot through the head on the fanciest sailboat you've ever seen."

"Poor man," she said. "What made him turn? Money?"

"Yeah. He grew up in poverty, then excelled in college. He should have stuck with law school, but I imagine that's when opportunity came knocking, and he couldn't resist."

David saw that Paula was beginning to nod off.

"I'm not leaving you tonight, honey, so don't worry. You scared the liver out of me today. I did the 11:00 news from the jail for WOOT. I didn't want us to get scooped. Just the bare essentials about Fullmer's arrest."

"But how are you going to sleep? There's no recliner, no bed. You need sleep. I think it's almost morning, anyway."

"Did I ever tell you I have a lovely baritone singing voice?"

"You're going to sing to me?"

"You bet."

He edged into her bed and pulled her up so he could embrace her while holding her against his chest. Then he began to hum the beautiful melody Dvorak had written so many years ago. He sang, *I am going home/It's not far, just close by/Through an open door/work all done, care laid by/Never fear no more.*"

Tears spilled down her cheeks.

CHAPTER THIRTY-EIGHT

This news story was even bigger than their last one.

David began by telling the story of Paula's kidnapping at age nine, the brutality she suffered, and her subsequent memory loss and induction into WITSEC.

Paula picked up the story with the murder of Marshal Sutherland as he was coming to unveil the truth after the death of her parents. She followed that with the attempts made on her life, and her decision to try hypnosis and therapy so she could find out who wanted her dead.

David took over, explaining how they had decided this experiment was harmful to her. He detailed their decision to go to LA and the first attempt on their life there.

As a special guest, they brought in Special Agent Moreno who told the rest of the story including the Federal indictments that had been handed down on Porter and Fullmer who, after their trial and conviction, would be in Terre Haute Federal prison in Indiana. He said he couldn't speculate on their sentencing, but the government was going for the death penalty.

Paula concluded.

"Other cells of their drug operations have been disbanded in Nevada, Utah, and Arizona. A substantial operation here in Chicago has been brought down.

"This brings to a satisfactory close a very bitter chapter in my early life. I am so thankful to Agent Moreno for his efforts to rescue me from two horrific kidnappings. I also owe a great debt to WOOT for their support of this investigation, and, of course, to David van Pelt who partnered with me and took his own share of knocks before we finally got to the truth.

"My takeaway from this? When your children are old enough to understand hard things, carefully tell them the truth about anything hard in your life that you have been trying to protect them from. Don't keep secrets that can wake up and destroy their lives after you are gone."

Mr. Q was exceedingly pleased with the results of their investigation and promoted Paula to full investigative co-anchor with David, which he was very happy about.

* * *

David celebrated their coup by buying a sailboat. He took Paula out on Lake Michigan for the maiden voyage. The summer day was hot on their backs, but the breeze cooled their faces. They were both very glad to be back home in Chicago.

"So, my dearest, what name have you decided upon?

"Which name do you like best?" she asked, still uncertain of her preference.

"If I had to live my life with one of them, I would probably choose Paula, because that is the name of the woman I fell in love with."

"Oh . . . David. You're sure?"

"About the love part or the name part?"

"Both."

"Yeah. I've been sure for a long time. Now that I have your full attention, let me just say that I can't think of anyone I would rather go from port to starboard with than you. Will you marry me, Paula James?"

"In a heartbeat. You must realize that this is what I've been angling for all along. You were just kind of slow to the party."

"Not as slow as you think."

Paula's heart did a Snoopy dance.

"What does that mean?"

"I'll never tell," he said.

He kissed her in the way that both thrilled her and melted any possible resistance.

"You've got yourself a deal," she said and decided to get in another kiss before the wind changed.

The End

OTHER BOOKS BY G.G. VANDAGRIFF

ROMANTIC SUSPENSE

Breaking News
Sleeping Secrets
Balkan Echo

REGENCY ROMANCE

His Mysterious Lady
Her Fateful Debut
Not an Ordinary Baronet
Love Unexpected
*
Lord Grenville's Choice
Lord John's Dilemma
Lord Basingstoke's Downfall
*
The Duke's Undoing
The Taming of Lady Kate
Miss Braithwaite's Secret
Rescuing Rosalind
Lord Trowbridge's Angel
The Baron and the Bluestocking

*

Much Ado about Lavender
Spring in Hyde Park (anthology)

HISTORICAL NOVELS

The Last Waltz: A Novel of Love and War
Exile
Defiance

WOMEN'S FICTION

The Only Way to Paradise
Pieces of Paris

GENEALOGICAL MYSTERIES

Cankered Roots
Of Deadly Descent
Tangled Roots
Poisoned Pedigree
The Hidden Branch

NON-FICTION

Deliverance from Depression
Voices In Your Blood

ABOUT THE AUTHOR

I realize that I am one of those rare people in the world who gets to live a life full of passion, suspense, angst, fulfillment, humor, and mystery. I am a writer. Every day when I sit down to my computer, I enter into a world of my own making. I am in the head of a panoply of characters ranging from a nineteen-year-old Austrian debutante (The Last Waltz) to a raging psychopath (The Arthurian Omen). Then there are the sassy heroines of my Regency romances . . .

How did this come about? I think I was wired to be a writer when I was born. There were a lot of things about my surroundings that I couldn't control during my growing up years, so I retreated to whatever alternate existence I was creating. The habit stuck, and now my family finds themselves living in my current reality during dinnertime as I overflow with enthusiasm about Wales, Austria, Italy, Regency England, or World War II. My latest craze is Bosnia.

Formerly a traditionally published, award-winning author, I went Indie in 2012. In that time I have become an Amazon #1 best-selling author of Regency romances. I enjoy genre-hopping, having published a genealogical mystery series, two women's fiction novels, three historical romances, three romantic suspense novels, thirteen Regency romances, some novellas, and a couple of non-fiction offerings.

With a BA from Stanford and an MA from George Washington University in International Relations, I somehow stumbled into finance. But, once my husband was through law school, I never wanted to do anything but write and raise kids. Now the kids are gone, but (even better) there are seven grandchildren who provide my rewards for finishing a manuscript.

Aside from the grandchildren, my favorite things include: Florence, Italy; snow storms; the Chicago Cubs; Oreos; real hot chocolate; Sundance Resort; lilacs; and dachshunds.

You can visit my website at ggvandagriff.com, follow me on Facebook or check out my Author Page on Facebook. Also, please follow me on Bookbub!

Sleeping Secrets
Copyright © 2018
by G.G. Vandagriff
All Rights Reserved

All rights reserved. No part of this book may be reproduced in any form or by any electronic
or mechanical means including information storage and retrieval systems, without
permission in writing from the author. The only exception is by a reviewer, who may quote
short excerpts in a review.
This book is a work of fiction. Names, characters, places, and incidents either are products
of the author's imagination or are used fictitiously. Any resemblance to actual persons,
living or dead, events, or locales is entirely coincidental.
G.G. Vandagriff
Visit my website at www.ggvandagriff.com
Printed in the United States of America
First Printing: December 2018
OW Press

29869952R00090

Made in the USA
San Bernardino, CA
18 March 2019